(M)OTHERING

(M)OTHERING

an anthology

edited by **Anne Sorbie and Heidi Grogan**

INANNA poetry & fiction

Toronto, Ontario, Canada
www.inanna.ca

We gratefully acknowledge the support of the Canada Council for the Arts and the Ontario Arts Council for our publishing program. We also acknowledge the financial support of the Government of Canada.

Front cover design: Val Fullard

Library and Archives Canada Cataloguing in Publication

Title: (M)othering : an anthology / edited by Anne Sorbie and Heidi Grogan.
Other titles: (M)othering (2022) | Othering
Names: Sorbie, Anne, 1960- editor. | Grogan, Heidi, editor.
Series: Inanna poetry & fiction series.
Description: Series statement: Inanna poetry & fiction
Identifiers: Canadiana (print) 20220188025 | Canadiana (ebook) 20220188351 | ISBN 9781771339124 (softcover) | ISBN 9781771339131 (HTML) | ISBN 9781771339148 (PDF)
Subjects: LCSH: Motherhood—Literary collections. | LCSH: Mothers—Literary collections. | CSH: Canadian literature (English)—21st century. | LCGFT: Poetry. | LCGFT: Short stories.
Classification: LCC PS8237.M64 M68 2022 | DDC C810.8/035252—dc23

Printed and Bound in Canada.

Published in Canada by
Inanna Publications and Education Inc.
210 Founders College, York University
4700 Keele Street, Toronto, Ontario M3J 1P3
Telephone: (416) 736-5356 Fax (416) 736-5765
Email: inanna.publications@inanna.ca Website: www.inanna.ca

Contents

Introduction

(M)OTHERING IS A UNIVERSALLY understood phenomenon that speaks to the act of becoming something unexpected and entirely outside ourselves. And this book is a collection of writing and art about that. On these pages, fifty-seven contributors illuminate the kind of gritty, body mind soul transformations that only the mothering myth can evoke. Their work will take you to wonder and wildness, kindness, beauty, grief, love. This book encompasses written and visual work that questions the act of mothering another human being… whether or not the individual in the mothering role is, in a traditional way, a mother at all.

These writers and artists show us what it means to create, to birth something, to love it, to suffer loss, to let go. They share their truths about trans-generational trauma. Some write of broken women, mothering their mothers and sisters, choosing not to be mothers. Having many mothers. Mothering grown children. Men who want to be mothered. Others tackle identity, adoption, abortion, addiction, self-care, sacrifice, nature and nurture, making art, unravelling, invention, loneliness, anger, laughter and joy. They are queer, Métis, Indigenous, French, male, Jewish, Mennonite, descendants of the Niisitapi (Blackfoot) and the Cree, settlers and immigrants. In unison, they speak about experiences far beyond the pathologizing of the pregnant female body.

The poetry, prose and art in the *(M)othering* anthology are presented and arranged as if part of an open conversation. A flow and an exchange begins with Sheri-D Wilson's "Mother," a poem in which we are invited to consider the anthropology of our subject, to stand with her at a liminal line where ambiguity and disorientation reign. The dialogue that follows is a sharing of authenticity, bravery and vulnerability; a discourse moving through states of being to Katherena Vermette's "egg," Joan Crate's "Song of the Seven Eves," Mary Warren Foulk's "Vision" and Amy Dryer's painting, "The Night Time Rituals." Marie-Manon Corbeil offers "As (M)other As Artist" and signals a great void when she says, "Between sadness and hope, there was art." What she proposes is taken up and answered/echoed later in "Date Night," by artist Kyle Nylund. His figure drips mother-blood.

Mothering is neither a linear experience nor easily confined to a consistent form practised by all who mother/care for their siblings, parents, their colleagues and friends or their children. To that end, the arrangement of works continues as an exploration rather than a traditional arrangement of genre and subject, and you, the reader, are invited to engage with the contributors in the demystification of mothering. Sanita Fejzić, in concert with the artist Ambivalently Yours, speaks to raising a child with her wife, and Kelly S. Thompson to caring for her dying sister. Joan Shillington's beautiful "Daughters" takes us to the image of water, to "oceans swoosh," to "sand, stones." Barb Howard's "Bigfoot Therapy," to the strangeness and disorientation of the empty nest, while Chynna Laird and Penney Kome speak to the generations of love that filled their experiences of being mothered. Rona Altrows takes us to 1974 and the kind of deeply flawed, institutional bias within which mothers were expected to function. Yvonne Trainer moves us, to and within "Halifax Public Gardens," and Aritha van Herk to the hilarious and "The Unfathomable Attraction of the Man Who Wants a Mother."

(M)othering concludes with Natalie Meisner's poem, "Left Me Open." "How much meaning / can one word hold" her first two lines ask. Indeed, how much meaning can one word, one act, one "change" in identity encode?

Ultimately, you, the reader, and all who have mothered and been mothered, will answer that question. On these pages, fifty-seven writers and artists are grateful, wounded, elated, limping, filled with sadness and joy. They come to us with wounds shining. Their truths, words and images attest to how mothering shatters and shapes us oh-so-dreadfully and oh-so-wondrously.

The skilled panoply of styles published here, both written and visual, are from contributors who reside in North America from Vancouver to Tucson, Toronto to Santa Fe, and places in between. They speak to the experience of what it means to create, to love, to be devastated and to share truths about who they/we are.

They stand in the belly of her/their/his/story. They are where they come from, what they've experienced, what they've created. Their work expresses and illuminates not only the kind of body, mind and soul search that the mothering myth evokes. Their work speaks—and loudly—to the fact that we are all othered in some way. This book belongs; it is theirs and yours and ours.

Anne Sorbie and Heidi Grogan

Le Pèlerinage
Sabine Lecorre-Moore & Patricia Lortie

Mother
Sheri-D Wilson

let me name this place
incognito,
for it is no place at all,
no one may claim it
as their own

no one owns this place,
we are all visitors here,
we all came from nothing
but spirit and star

let us listen to the wind in the trees
naked as a cloudless sky,
for she will tell us
everything we need to know
about ourselves.

here now,
my tongue is parched
dry as sun bone sand,
I gag on the burning land
I once hoped to unearth

discover at my root,
the hourglass is shattered
I cannot find the past

stripped of my name,
my heart,
my place
and my womb.

mother, I'm balancing on the discord
of an unknown quest.

mother, may I have a choice?

yes, you may
choose the choice
to save this place
but you cannot own anything

a seed is not a flower, a
drop is not a stream, a
tree is not a forest, to
sleep is not to dream.

mother, how on earth
can I birth a child into this rot?

child, from your first breath
to your last, you will be sorry
and I am sorry for that,
please know, once you make the choice,
you make the choice
for life.

I make this choice for you, mother
there is no ancestral right,
I live with the choices
I make

in life
I own nothing,
nothing owns me.

My conscience will bow to you
when there is not enough
water to drink,
My conscience will bow to you
when there is not enough
food to eat,

I vow to bow to you, mother
in your devastation

what is life
when so much has been taken?

mother, may I love you?

       child, life begins
       with a breath
       listen as I exhale
       through the leaves—
       you are not alone

mother wave water
mother tide moon
mother sun ocean earth
as gone as everything holy

I feel the waters rising

mother, may I
live?

Toward Hygge[1]
Vivian Hansen

Where the Me becomes We,
like a slow saunter,
hand in hand toward a candlelit supper for two.
Like a ring of hands held,
around a pine tree in Canmore,
to sing and dance as the Winter Solstice passes.

In my sixtieth year, which also happens to correspond with Canada's
    150th birthday,
I am walking toward solstice
and offer a backward glance to women before me.
Mother and grandmother, my Danish Bedstemor.[2]
They should be more than a backward glance.
They should be more than old breasts that map my DNA,
my forward motion in Canada.
They are cloven on the inside
because of immigration.
Their tongues split in two, Danish and English.

The way tongues grow together after a piercing.
My women conquer the cleaving. They seek hygge,
how it might dance in this new land.

> Bedstemor has been working for weeks now on a Sengeteppe,[3]
> a bedspread white and light and heavy as spring snow.
> She prepares squares
> of a lacy snowflake pattern,
> all of which will be bound together
> in a final large spread.

---

[1] A place of comfort; a verb of Being.
[2] Formal name for Grandmother.
[3] A blanket for the bed.

As each square is completed,
Bedstefar[4] asks: *Har du gøre færdig med en andet fire-kante,*
    lille mor?
Have you finished another square, little mother?

He loves to watch her ebony eyes that she will mostly entrust
to the white squall of crochet.
Then, as her eyes
turn to him, she offers two black pools.

Square is too simple.
It is design, four elemental corners of knowing.
This is håndearbeje/handiwork. The prayer of hands
imitates God's design in four;
a quatrain of purpose; an impulse of links.

      Hvem er du gør sengeteppe for? asks Bedstefar.
      Who are you making the sengeteppe for?

For one of her girls. Whoever will need it the most.
She says this to avoid prophecy: naming one
of her daughters as someday needing—more than the other.
There are things that cannot be. Until they are.

Eldest Anna, husband Eduard and two sons
prepare for immigration.
Anna despairs, a fear she might abandon hygge.

      All I want is our home here,[5]
    our own furniture that we have had for years.
      I know it is not fancy, but it is ours!
Our hygge. And so is the garden, my flowers and plants.
      It is precious to me, don't you see?

---

[4] Formal name for Grandfather.
[5] Memoirs of Anna Hansen, October 25, 1960 (unpublished).

Bedstemor's Sengeteppe hangs in lush white lengths across a bed.
It is a rich thing that gropes for endings,
relaxing its links over the four corners.
The cotton is sturdy and heavy
like almond icing.
The Sengeteppe collects air, wind, fire, and water.

Air, for the scent of firewood and peat burning, settling into
tough strands that Bedstemor linked.
Fire, for the passion between them, the faith that keeps them whole,
while storms rage around them.
Water, for unseen mists in Danish autumns.
Earth, for what is and what shall be, if there is blessing.

Hygge is the moment where You become We
as we lay beneath four elements.

When her daughter, son-in-law, and grandsons prepare to leave,
Bedstemor gathers the Sengeteppe into a box to give to Anna.
This daughter will need it the most.

Ship route: Le Havre, Southampton, Montreal

Anna's tears become the ocean.
Despondent waters with no vision but grey.

This is too horrible.
I may as well plunge into the deep of the ocean
so the hawks can have me, I am no good anyway so why not?
I staggered along the corridor of the ship
around the corner of the boathys [sic]
only 2–3 yards from the railings.
And who was standing right there? Eduard.
And I run straight into his arms and believe me, it felt good.[6]

---

[6] Memoirs of Anna Hansen, October 25, 1960.

My mother is tall enough to wave the white bedspread like a flag over the bed. Its cloth settles like a prairie snowstorm. I plant my little self on the opposite side of her. In a housework dance between the two of us, we smooth down the links and white ropes of cotton, taking care to make it flat and beautiful, like a field of snow dreams. This repetition, this routine, is a pattern that I know as a fresh movement each day. A little girl must learn how to find hygge.

Anna once pleaded for answers from her parents.
What to do about the desperate loneliness on a flat.flat prairie.
The mountains so close—stone refusing hygge.
Bedstemor offered more words: what you don't know and don't
      understand, leave it.
Live your life with what you know.

What you know is hygge;
the struggle with ephemera, realize that new things require a name
in English.
The cleavage of the tongue closes in on itself, after the pierce.
Sengeteppe. Bedspread. That Hygge Thing that warms the We of Us.

I pluck a Colour Life paint chip bookmark
from a book I am reading.
It is a yellow called 'Faceless,'
so light as to be the breath of a moon.
So subtle but intrusive, so that one may never notice the law of it;
how it couples with light, and lies down
in a slumber where skin strokes a moonlight.
It is hygge that holds the mtDNA of yellow, so distant
in mother-generations. Its milk perceived
only in mitochondrial tones.
If I lie down with this colour,
I will sleep in deep alpha bones—knogler.[7]

---

[7] Bones. Also the root word of "knowledge," where the bones were cast for divination.

8

Anna says: *I am repairing the Sengeteppe.*
There was so much dust and dirt in it, I was afraid it would fall apart.
But it hung together.
Dad strung it over a clothesline in the basement,
then stitched and repaired some of the holes in it.
Bedstemor said it must go to whoever needed it the most.
Anna is never happier than when she binds old mysteries together.
She decides to release some of her power.

This is what a Crone does when she senses
the end of things.
Repair may be in order.

I covet the Sengeteppe.
I want its heft and hard feel
of its links in my lap, on my bed.
I want the fingertip stretch between myself
and my Bedstemor, like Michelangelo's painting:
God touching the soul of Adam, fingertip to fingertip.

Anna gives it to me. Watches my eyes for signs of delight.
My hands stroke the crochet links,
making smooth the white lines that sometimes mound
over a bed. All my life I've curled my fingers in between
my Bedstemor's håndearbejde squares in my sleep, covered by
    her prayers.
Only now do I begin to see patterns, geometrics of hope,
all fabrics and fabrications turning
and imposing angles of life—toward hygge.

Mange tak, Bedstemor. Many thanks.
I whisper to the air, to her, listening.
In the place where I speak, Bedstemor smiles.
Each crochet link is a path, a trail of homilies
for mothers who were broken by immigration.

In this Canada, hygge divines
a place of rest.

My daughter stands in the bedroom doorway as my voice stumbles
over words that tell her this story.
I needed the Sengeteppe the most.
I belay this word so her ears absorb it as a necessary noun;
a link to her great-grandmother.
I needed the Sengeteppe the most.
Not my mother, my sister, my aunt, my cousin. Me.

That's a beautiful story, mom.
Her long fingers stroke the old Sengeteppe, slide along its re-stitched links.
Her touch is a dialect between herself and her mothers.
I seek her face, her black eyes, to catch a hint of her thoughts.
She looks back at me, smiling. *Hygge.*
That word reminds me of hug.
Her eyes glisten like the old woman who made the Sengeteppe,

those black stones, gleaming
under a slow creek of tears.

The Crossing
Norma Kerby

did you weep before you
stepped into the dinghy

did your dry mouth moan as
you clutched her hand tighter

was drowning less a tragedy
than the horrors left behind

in the mother other robes you wore through underworlds of
      persecution   torture   slavery   genital mutilation
you could not bear to think of her laughing smile smashed

was that the risk your other mother mind
      tried to snatch from darkness

a void in which you hid your fractured soul
imprisoned until that shore of last decision

      non-life in cold sea sinking
her fine black hair spread wide like waves

All in a Day's Work
Lori D. Roadhouse

Today
a child tells me,
      my new baby sister is living
      in the clouds now.
My knees buckle
this child is so matter-of-fact
with this blunt force trauma of life and death,
a fact that few adults can face with such honesty
openness and innocence.

Today
a child tells me,
      a boy was bullying me
      and it made me feel kind of sad
      and mad,
and then with a feisty twinkle says,
      Because you're supposed to be mad at them!
It takes my breath away,
her insight and wisdom,
her self-esteem blossoming before me
as she shares this tidbit of playground street smarts.

Today
a child tells me,
      I was scared when I couldn't find my mom
      but then she came home when it was dark
      and I didn't tell her that I was hungry
      because she was sad.
My heart breaks
for his empathy and maturity,
his isolation and emptiness,
how old his soul is in first grade.

Today
a child tells me,
       when I was little my daddy threw me
       and I hit my head against the wall
       so we moved and that's why my name is changed
       because we don't like him anymore.
And my soul shatters
for his,
already precarious,
running scared from living demons
who are supposed to protect him.

Today
a child tells me,
       Teacher, I love you.
And my heart swells
because I know this child
is grasping,
needing and wanting
something that has been out of her reach
for most of her six years.

My eyes meet hers,
face value,
no hesitation.
I reply
       I love you, too.

Children of the Forest
Patricia Lortie

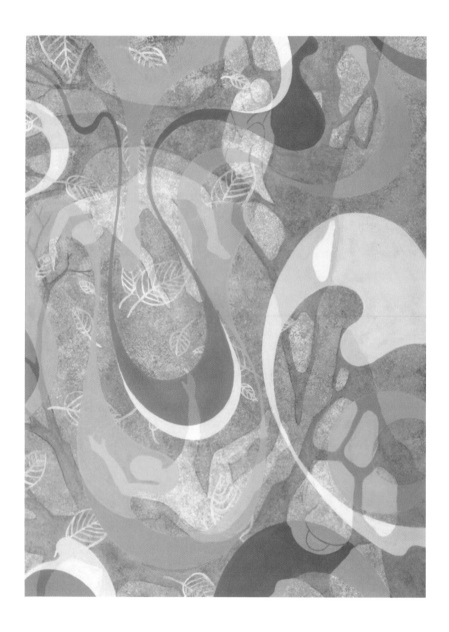

First Want 1963
Joan Shillington

Lauretta opens the door wide at my unexpected visit
while wandering the beach road, ushers me in,
asks if I would like ripple chips and apple juice,
my favourite treat she keeps for me.
Her friend Bette pours coffee.
Working women, red nails, matching blouses, slacks.
Discuss their desire for a baby, to *just get pregnant!*
Twelve years old I crunch and listen
to the first thirst of want in my life.
They question birth control pill problems, sexual revolution.
Did the Pope have a point? When and if the time comes,
no yellow room or clothes. Breast or bottle?

I dip my chips in the juice.
Minimize the crunch.

egg
Katherena Vermette

she is waiting
she is
a swollen belly
housed in soft bones
waiting
wrapped in glowing skin
waiting
a child in june
waiting
an infant
an egg
waiting
for just the perfect
moment
to crack

Latch
Jessica Gigot

for Jeanine

The lamb, four minutes old
stumbles toward the scent
of safety, vacant womb.
Lurking in barn shadows,
I hesitate to intervene
believing this nascent soul
will find its way.

The lamb, forty minutes old
stands and knocks the bag
with a steady jolt.
Despite the wet chill
of March and amniotic fluid
mouth discovers milk.

I come back to the house
before dawn to warm up.
In the privacy of a shower
I circle my tender, dark areolae
now larger than a silver dollar.

When you finally arrive, I hope
you latch on to me without fear.
Let me nourish you
with all the flavor
my world can offer.

Song of the Seven Eves
Joan Crate

"A scientist at Oxford University released details of a project that
claims almost everyone living in Europe can trace an unbroken
genetic link to one of only seven prehistoric women…"
(*Globe & Mail*, F-8, May 26, 2001)

In ancient Africa, they were earth
and root hung on mountain ranges,
stretched over flatlands of belly
and back, dug into pits of instinct.

Bone knitters and skin stretchers,
the dirty mothers pieced together
a human world in the wilds of their wombs
their mitochondria swimming body

to body through ages of swamp and ice,
hitchhikers riding from feral to civil,
barefoot survival to a gluttonous
century of emissions, fast food, disposable

single-use, unfixable, trending, tired,
updated, replaceable, chipped, hacked,
contaminated, indestructible
everything.

       Foremothers fed us milk and need,
flowering love, harrowing pain made flesh,
cell locked to primitive cell, rib stacked on rib.
Forbidden fruit in their mouths and bellies,
they delivered a feast of sacrificial lambs,
scapegoats and predators
while mouthing a language of curse
and prospect. In sickness, holes, peril

and stupor they whispered their cravings—
more smouldering coals of heat,
more slurps of marsh water, *more*
mouthfuls of roots and rodents—

into fetuses multiplying like Ponzi schemes
through wilderness brains. *More*
they howled and their children and
their children's children, an incessant

longing for drink, snacks, gadgets
and glee—first need then desire
then greed—breeding *more* demands
in drought, deluge, sickness and famine.

We became a race of dreamers
waking drugged nightmares
in smog-dead daylight and electric night,
a chorus of debt-ridden consumers

demanding *more* status symbols
and throw-away dishes, mass
producers progressively putting out
                    more, more, more

the planet.

The Pregnancy Poems
Joan Crate

I. During the Fertility Ritual

we wish air and fire, pour water
on earth and speak our wish
to four winds. We ask for a multiplicity

of cells, a blueprint
to shape an upper lip, flare
a nostril or fold into hands a talent
for piano or mime or implanting life
in a ball of clay.

Three mothers press around
the young woman with an empty womb,
our minds pushing out a dream
to plant in tomorrow.

Let them be—
life's cry, our wish, this expectation
that is old and new and the best of us.

Let it be.

II. Snowball Effect

The union of hydrogen, oxygen
and cold creates a ballet of feathers
spinning

       gathering. The ground
shifts. It could be wind, an unstable
foothold or human hand crushing

breath from a fistful of grace.

Anomaly. Initiation. A snowball
starts rolling downhill

gathers itself cell to cell
moves toward a destination
nine months long.

                She grows bigger
heavier, falls outside herself
into the choreography of veins and organs

reaches to a sea of stars
rushing to light, the pierce of pain.
Imagine

     an eggshell breaking
open on the yellow sun, a new life
full, raw, unfolding—

III. Rock-a-bye

And she is Sisyphus
pushing a stone uphill day after day.

Her purpose is to safely deliver
her present to the future, but the situation
has gone from possibility to nausea,
from a pebble to a planet as inextricable
from her body as breath.

Moment by moment she shifts—
a student of physics citing *mass* and *energy*,
an accountant balancing a spreadsheet,
a musician orchestrating muscle and tendon—
duelling banjos—playing everything from spring's

lamb-fleeced crocuses and three-watt sun
to summer's gold-ringed fingers
and a pear of light.

IV. Making Bread

A lump of dough rises
in the kitchen with a wide-open door,
the summer air oven-warm.

We've been hungry nine months
for a loaf of tomorrow, aroma drifting
through a house of arms and need.

Cinnamon and sugar fall from fingers,
spinning a moon, a star. At night we rock
a small universe to sleep in our dreams.

Vision
Mary Warren Foulk

On the day our daughter is born,
at an urban hospital outside Portland,
a family appears at the window.
Such awe of concrete and wildlife,
the tender prayer I need as the epidural
numbs waves of fraught labour.
Sixteen hours and a C-section later,
our daughter floats in my wife's arms.
Ten fingers, ten toes?
I ask from below a fog.
She is an answer I longed for
in this fragile state of becoming mother
while motherless.

Two white-tailed deer emerge quietly,
like spirits at dusk.
Mother and child eat fallen leaves
dusted with fresh snow.
They stare curiously, humbly,
through the thin glass
that separates us.
The mother grazes slowly,
her ears velvet and
taut, while the fawn,
its winter coat of grayish brown,
plays in wooded shadows.
Each visit a sign:
the loved ones are near and still.

I understand the doe's eyes,
darkened with awareness.

First Day
Katherine Matiko

i   we sleep swaddled in separate beds
carefully breathing this new air

ii   her name, like her blankets, won't stick
I struggle to remember it when asked

I lift her from a tangle of linens
and christen her woman child

iii   arms and mouth her antennae
she searches blindly   frantic
leaves a snail's trail on my neck
sniffs the areola   calms
takes me in her mouth
then arches away   satiated
curls on my chest
a turtle out of its shell

iv   stroking her skin is like reaching down
to tap the surface of a pond
her breath on my face is the earth
crushed beneath me as I kneel
I place my lips where the sun reflects
and drink deep drink deep

Birthright
Kelly Kaur

Mummy sits in the corner of the room
dupatta over her head
hands in clasped obeisance
murmuring verses from the *Adi Granth*

I scream in unbearable agony
expelling this errant child from my womb

her prayers don't make a difference
to the intense pain
but her presence in the hospital room
calms my soul

At that precise cross point
I envision my mother's birth
I remember my birth
I finally give birth

my daughter's rebellious cries fill the room
rising to a crescendo to greet my mother's chants

three generations of women
three continents
forever
inextricably linked

How I Finally Became a Mom

Jennifer Carr

I.

Seasons came and went
as did fifteen years of my life
During that time I was told
some people are not born to be a mom
that I was not born to be a mother

I heard that lie so many times
I convinced myself of that truth
Like inmates convicted for crimes
they believed they didn't commit

I believed I was no better than those convicted
Those convicted in her eyes

Incarcerated in her crippling care
was the cage that clipped my wings
stopped my dreams mid-flight

The yard where I yearned to feel the sun
showed me
the sky is never the limit
but
I could not see past the bars
she enslaved me in

And yet I loved her

And would have died for her
In fact I almost did several times

II.

After death comes rebirth

Then comes that newfound hope
a hope which brings courage

Suddenly I had no fear
It took me six months
of carefully laid-out plans
to plan my escape route.

But it paid off

It all paid off

I broke free from that cage
and learned to fly once again

No more solitary confinement

III.

Seven years have passed
and the greatest gift
besides my freedom
is the sound of small feet
running around

That's right, I was born to be a mom
God knew all along
He would bless upon me two children
and
with their blessed hearts
they made me a mom

when the time was right
after I was able to leave
my jail cell behind

Some sentences
aren't mine to serve

Taking the Leap
Julianne Palumbo

They tell you not to lean too close to the edge
or you might fall off.
But sometimes falling
can be a good thing,
especially when it means
you've been reaching.
Like when you're trying to wipe
the smudge from a window's corner,
coax a bottle from the shelf
with the tips of your fingers,
or take a stranger's child into your home
to raise as your own.

Sometimes we need to fall
like the seed of a maple tree,
the way it spins to the ground
and embeds itself,
ready to become something more.

But I don't know how to look at the crevasse
and fear nothing—
the unknown traumas,
lurking behaviours,
horrors passed between generations.
Why do we take a large step
over a small gap?
Is it because the fall might be too steep?

Child, if I reach for your hand
will you take mine,
release the grip of your old life?
Will you hang on
even when my own footing
feels unsure?

Fostering Love
Julianne Palumbo

The way trees silhouette flat against a burning sky at dusk
pale like elephant skin when the sky turns black,

so too can giving love away leave you feeling   filled.
Each act of kindness a dopamine drip for the giver.

But sometimes doing something good can leave you feeling bad,
the way the lost get found
the way you can both weather the storm and be weathered by it.

They say *No good deed*…and all that jazz,
and so I find myself winnowing the good feelings from the bad,
trying to decide why my heart lacks rest,
why my love doesn't feel true.

This child, half boy, half man
hung up like a coat in the lost and found,
loose labels, missing tags,
just an unwoven thread among the stitching,
and I wonder if going through the motions can ever be enough.

The Night Time Rituals
Amy Dryer

The Night Time Rituals 2
Amy Dryer

Night rituals
are occasions of tears and silence
answered with time
and milk

My Life in Colours
Marie-Manon Corbeil

As (M)other as Artist
Marie-Manon Corbeil

PAINTING IS A FORM of expression that I came to after a long journey.

When I was thirty-six years old, I adopted an almost three-year-old from a Russian orphanage. I fell instantly in love with the little boy and he changed my life in remarkable ways.

Nineteen years later my husband and I learned that our son's biological mother drank alcohol during her pregnancy. Our son was diagnosed in 2018 with both Foetal Alcohol Syndrome Disorder (FASD) and Attention Deficit Hyperactivity Disorder (ADHD).

Over the years I suffered much alongside my son, from the kind of effects rejection and bullying have on the body and the mind, to the kind of extreme stresses that our school and medical systems are not equipped to handle or help with.

It was after almost losing my son, after almost giving up myself, that I began to paint. Slowly.

Between sadness and hope, there was art.

Today, art is my way of life. Not therapy, but something that provides much pleasure and satisfaction. I realize how lucky I am, that life's challenges and what I call its *cruel difficulties* provided me with an opportunity to accomplish in ways I never imagined I would…as (m)other…as artist.

Naissance
Dorothy Bentley

Pureté torn by Love's fool's gold.
She is barely awake; yet,
she believes what she's told.

Baby blooms, a new life planted.
Une grossesse qui choque, larmes
like her membrane with a scalpel.

Will her life be better, once
she gives her flesh to another?
Will stérile femme praise her
for making her a mother?

Some will call her héroïne
while others call her lâché,
but the one she holds in vigil,
is bébé de naissance who woke her.

Bloodline at the Water Cooler

Kim Mannix

An Ohio woman found her birth mother
smack in the middle of 9 to 5.
She worked a few floors down, same company,
same ugly t-shirt at the corporate picnics.

Were there whispered conversations
between DNA strands? Is there something
in the mitochondria, the hearts of our cells,
toiling to keep us in reach of what we need?
A nuclear beacon, reverberating
so we're never severed from our blood.

All the cities she could've gone to,
all the doors she could've pushed open,
leading to other doors, other corridors,
but she followed a maze of halls
that led right back to her beginning.
Umbilical navigation.
Decades long.

I want the math of this. Theorems,
numbers, not just to explain the odds,
but to offer the proof. The data of origin.
Diagrams of bonds, covalent and familial.

It happens
more often than you'd think.
It's changed the way I see everyone:
my daughter's teacher,
the neighbour two doors down,
forever clipping away at his hedge.
That cashier, whose cheekbones
cut close to my sister's.

What if all connections run deeper than we know?
What if chromosomes outwit the brain,
override chance and circumstance?

What if our bloodline always
draws itself into a circle?
Spinning, whirring, like test tubes
in a centrifuge—listen. Look out.
Anyone of us could be family.

Marsupiak
E. D. Morin

I ONCE WROTE A STORY about a man with a prosthetic womb. The man, Geo, is married to the head researcher at the pharmaceutical corporation where the device is being developed. The Marsupiak, in other words, is his wife's invention, and it is Soleil's desire that leads Geo to be fitted with the experimental device. Believing in the egalitarianism of marriage, Soleil convinces her husband that since she carried and birthed their now three-year-old daughter Ursa, it is his turn. But all of this is backstory. The real action is more mundane.

Geo and Ursa, whom he is caring for during his "confinement," go for a walk to the grocery store. As they walk, Geo experiences twinges of pain and is unable to carry his daughter, even when she begs him, even after she sits on the sidewalk and refuses to budge, so that Geo is forced to tug her along by the hand. On their return home, Ursa plays in the empty bathtub and then wanders into the couple's bedroom, the scene of her own conception. Then she finds Geo unconscious on the living room rug. She lies down, whimpering, not touching him as he is wet with amniotic fluid. Carry me, she cries.

The story, titled "Carry Me," was rejected by a handful of literary journals and then I shelved it. But it haunts me still. There's something bleak and ham-fisted about the work, and yet something in the tale feels ripe with possibility. Like so many abandoned stories, there's always a chance to revisit the work and discover ways to improve it. Sometimes with failed stories, lack of good editing is the trouble. Other times the narrative drags. And sometimes in failed stories, I locate the ragged edges of my psyche, dark places of prejudice and carelessness and outdated archetypes. What is it about Geo and Soleil's tale that won't let me go?

Maybe the story haunts me because of what it might say about me. About my entire, conflicted experience of motherhood. Entire? As if I am done with mothering. As if motherhood is ever truly done. Even as they approach their thirties, my daughter, my son, continue to want mothering.

The singular urge to parent arose when I was about twenty. A needing to hold, a sense of cradling a tiny someone. Where do such stirrings arise from? In retrospect, I suspect hormones or, more aptly, my lizard brain. Whatever its source, the yearning was most definitely NOT rational. I can't explain why I was suddenly so *sure* about my wanting. The third of six children, I'd had a reasonably happy childhood—until puberty struck and my mother fell ill. Watching my mother, it seemed that parenting had exacted a terrific cost. Further, I bore a deep sense of being ill-suited to motherhood. I'd long suspected that I was flawed in this regard and wondered if I could form a deep human connection with anyone. It seemed unlikely that I'd marry. What I really wanted was a career, a life of adventure, a life of discovery. Mostly I wanted to be a man, or at least to have what I'd long perceived men had. Marriage, if it ever transpired, was a distant planet. Mothering was beyond even those reaches. Most unlikely.

I can barely recall the circumstances preceding the urge, this wanting to hold. Was I returning from spending time with someone? One of the nerdy boys who occasionally asked me out? Or had I been alone? And where? Perhaps the university, working through math problems in a library carrel. What I do recall is walking home on the streets of south Edmonton, crossing a freeway bridge. Concrete underfoot, the edges of ragged green foliage in my peripheral vision. And then a brief tug, a glimmer pulsing through me. A stirring that left a lasting mark. From that stirring, that brief, crackling sense of cradling, I thought that, yes, I might be capable of raising a child. All at once I could imagine mothering. A feeling that I could love. That I was actually capable of loving and caring for someone. A child.

The audacity of that. Suddenly suited to motherhood, to riding out all that it might bring. That I might be a person who *wanted* a child. But how many? My thoughts spun to imagining two, no more than two, and in that I was prescient. And then, naively, wanting boys because hadn't being a girl disappointed in so many ways? I didn't want my children to experience that dysphoria.

What did I want, really?

At its core, "Carry Me" is a reversal story. Soleil, the career-minded workaholic. Geo, the pregnant stay-at-home dad. Even their names: woman as sun, man as earth. But I could see that in my efforts to topple the usual gender myths, I hadn't addressed much at all. I'd simply swapped the roles of husband and wife, had made the once-fertile Soleil masculine and all-powerful, had taken Geo, a former airline pilot, and grounded him, rendered him passive.

It strikes me now that I was merely echoing stories of Greek gods and other predictable tales that were part of the usual Western canon, the kinds of stories I'd been reading since childhood. Could I learn from these myths and carry them someplace new?

Perhaps the telling was the problem. Ursa as the narrator, a sometimes precocious, sometimes incomprehensible three-year-old. Ursa is able to sense that something is amiss in her world, but her voice is pure need. In this, nothing is resolved. Meanwhile, we learn little of Geo's motivations except that he is weakened and depressed. He misses being a pilot. He misses a more active life. He is losing his fight to bear a child.

What is left is Soleil, of whom we have glimpses. She does not appear physically, only through the narrator or spoken about in simplified conversations between Ursa and Geo in which, more often than not, Geo corrects what Ursa says. An example. The artificial womb he is fitted with, the marsupial *Marsupiak*, Ursa mistakenly calls the *Super Yak*. And another. When Ursa calls her mother, Soleil, an *expecutive*.

These fleeting details say more about Ursa and very little about Soleil and what drives her. What possesses Soleil to create such a device? Does she sense she's crossed an ethical line by having her husband test the Marsupiak? And what of the kangaroo dad and his daughter Ursa, the little bear?

Sometimes symbols flit through a writer's pen, through the synaptic taps on the keyboard. They surface unquestioned and then somehow survive the editing phase. But how do they belong in this story? And, perhaps more interesting, what do these symbols say about me? Which is why failed stories are such gifts. The possibility of sifting through the writing and discovering what's actually been transmitted. Asking myself, is this what I believe, is this what I mean to say? Or is it something I mechanically and unquestioningly carry around with me and deposit as I write? What is the truth anyway?

Searching for answers, I delve into the Greek myth of Callisto. There are multiple versions of the myth, but in one version Callisto appears as King Lycaon of Arcadia's daughter, a companion of Artemis sworn to virginity. The god Zeus disguises himself as Artemis and rapes Callisto. Out of this violent, fraudulent union a son is born, Arcas. When Zeus' wife Hera hears of her husband's misdeeds, she aims her jealous anger at Callisto and Arcas and transforms them into bears. The story comes full circle when the huntress Artemis kills the bear mother and son and exiles them skyward where they become Ursa Major and Ursa Minor, two very recognizable northern constellations.

Callisto, in another version of the myth, is a proficient knitter, able to fashion beautiful objects out of yarn. This is a gift too. In one scene, Ursa describes how Geo wove the living room rug out of discarded bits of climbing rope, another remnant of Geo's former, active life. That Geo fashioned the rope rug and that Ursa loves to play there. A universe unto itself, the rug is where Ursa weaves her own tales. The rope rug thus appears to symbolize a broken umbilical cord, a lifeline that fails to save the father or his unborn child. Ursa whimpers beside her father and wishes he would get up, she wishes he would carry her and hold her in his arms. Most of all, she wishes to supplant the being that grows inside the Marsupiak.

We want to believe that we are agents of our own destinies. We want to think that we choose our lives and our families. But no matter how much we think we choose, fate or chance or serendipity is writ large over our efforts at reproduction. Becoming a parent is all chance. How much can we even know about ourselves or the myriad possibilities of two people coming together? Reproduction. That supreme moment of inattention when the mammals in us supersede everything else, when our brains are turned OFF.

Arrogance. Hubris. To think we can control our biology. We might hope, but we will never make a child to order. We cannot replicate ourselves (barring cloning) nor would we truly want to, yet we also can't help but replicate ourselves in countless ways. We overlook our flaws and hope that the best of us will appear in our children, but we have no control over any of it. Our hopes for our children almost always miss the mark anyway. Instead, children surprise us in inexplicable ways, in ways that expand our human experience. This is the bear in our lives, the wild gift of our irrational, mammalian selves.

We exile the bear at our peril.

When I gave birth to my daughter, she entered the world face up. The delivery was long and difficult. A huge tear needed to be sewn up, and the blood loss was excessive. In the week following, I could barely rise without blacking out. Stitching this experience into my life, I told myself that my daughter had arrived face up, even though the more conventional face down would have been considerably easier on both of us, because she needed to see what was happening. She needed to witness her own arrival. I told myself that there was a moment in the delivery when our pubic bones formed two opposing triangles that made a butterfly. This whimsical and unscientific tale helped me find the beauty in her difficult birth.

Mothering my daughter, I would learn so much more.

I had wished for sons, as if wishing made a difference to the outcome, as if gender even mattered. But that was my thinking at the time. Having been raised in the binary, I was still stuck in the binary. The truth is, at the moment of birth, all I cared about was a child, a healthy living child. And now I know the true gift of mothering a daughter, how she's shaped me. She humbles me with her grace and intellect, her profound understanding of the world, the love she inspires in me. A life without her is unimaginable.

The child takes a part of you, many parts. If you choose mothering and make this decision willingly, as I did, you inevitably find yourself asking during moments of sheer exhaustion and depletion, what was I thinking? Why did I want this? And then you try to imagine a life without mothering, without your remarkable children. You can't. I can't.

As a parent, I gained a true sense of my limits, a sense of how I would cope when those limits were badly exceeded, which was often. I developed capacities I didn't know I lacked. I gained a better understanding of my own mother and how hard I'd been on her in my youth. The cost of parenting has sometimes felt great. But I'm a better person for it.

Here's another Greek myth about a bear. When Atalanta is born, her father Iasus abandons her on a mountaintop because she is a girl and what he'd wanted was a boy. A she-bear discovers Atalanta and suckles her, and then a hunter finds the child and raises her. Atalanta grows to be a huntress herself, as swift-footed as Artemis. Through the she-bear's nurturing intervention, Atalanta comes into herself and discovers her own capacities, her own wildness. Later, Iasus and Atalanta are favourably reunited. I imagine the possibilities.

I imagine the possibilities of another Soleil.

Mother3
Ambivalently Yours

(M)other
Sanita Fejzić

You were born past midnight
      after the alarm bell cut the night in two

           —caesarian—

      at 10.3 pounds
          our big gift.

The doctor, a man whose head resembles the colour of a blank
sheet of paper
      wearing brand-name *Hunter* boots of the same frosted blush
lifted you up as if with holy hands, in prayer,
      "Born on Christmas day and he hath no father."
His words, spoken in a fake British accent betrayed an old mentality.

On your birth certificate my name fills the space of "father/
other parent."
      I am your other mother, your (m)other, but there was only
room for one on the page.

In kindergarten at the Waldorf school
      where the prime minister's children go to learn
two older boys   zoomed   across   the hallway
like   arrows
 "Haha—t'as pas de papa!"
      Their words hit me in the chest: ha!   ha!
pa!   pa!   pa!
They darted by   pa!   papa!
When I asked the teacher to talk to them she said, "They're just children."
      So are you, my son.

A year later, the principal of your new school suggested
      I put you in karate
so you could have a "proper father figure"

                              "a sensei"

                                    "a man."

I try not to get tired of explaining.
No: there is no father.
It's not that hard.
You only have mothers.
Anonymous sperm donor, yes.
No: no: no: my brother is absolutely not like your father. He is
your uncle.
Just like how other people's uncles are not their fathers. (Do I really
need to explain this?)

At night, we compare beauty marks in the mirror

        our bodies punctuated by little islands of beautiful
singularities
we find one in common on our chin—this random physical trait that
unites us, mother & child.

Mother2
Ambivalently Yours

And even though you don't have my genes or DNA
my sun   you have   all my love   dedication
delicate attention
          always & always into infinity

and even though
          on your birth certificate my name fills the space of "father/
other parent"
                    I am your other mother, your (m)other
the one that's learning to be light
          to laugh when others look for a father
like that time I made you giggle at Toys Я Us
          holding up a mask of Padmé Amidala to my face
                    exhaling in a deeply performative tone:
                              "I Am Your (M)other."

Night's Waking
Mary Warren Foulk

Did I hear the doors lock,
the cold metal sync?
Did I draw the curtains,
thwart the neighbour's watchful
eye? Did I turn off the stove,
align the knobs to
Off Off Off?
Did I feed the cats, both
the one staring at me
with her yellow eyes
and the one nestled next to you,
keeping time with your snoring,
her purr a heavy rasp,
a dying elder we rescued,
namely to rescue us.
Did I tell you I love you,
even say good night?
Did I listen for the children's
breath, lean my face next to theirs,
close, to stare at their
dreaming, wonder why they don't hear
these questions and other noises—
the lone owl singing
atop the shadowing pines.
Did I add to tomorrow's lists—
what already I have forgotten?
Tasks streaked by the bathroom
mirror, torn and
yellowing. Will it ever be dawn
and will enough ever
be enough?

37 Dustballs
Norma Kerby

i didn't mean to count them   the dustballs that is
but in the tedium of keeping bubonic plague
from skittering down the hallway and
consuming my children
i started to count the enemy
forgetting those sweet rewards of
being a mother   a single mother
        a single mother without
              a vacuum cleaner that works

a mother is better than a vacuum cleaner
she does not require electricity or   valentine's cards
or boxes of chocolates   although if i hid them
        the chocolates that is   under the bed
a terrifying squad of miniature lint lovers
would ferret them out   rush towards me
covered with snakes of dog hairs and cat hairs
and flakes of aging skin   all wrapped together

Mum! Mum! Mum! Look what we found!

treasures   pirate treasures   treasures i had forgotten
they hide under the bed with my dreams and my youth
captured alive by that dustmongering never-ending
hollering pack of dustball busters bursting with joy

what was i to say as we sat down together and ate them
every last one

Reason
Katherine Smart

THERE'S A FORM in the principal's office with accusatory little boxes for parents to complete when their children are late. I haven't seen the form but I've heard about it from other schoolyard mothers who say the boxes are small and demanding. I don't understand what I could possibly write about being late that would actually fit.

This morning my husband left early because he had a dentist appointment before work so my five-year-old got herself dressed but then rolled on the dog's bed in her black pants and the dog is white so I wiped the hair off with a damp cloth because I couldn't find one of the five Costco lint rollers and then her pants were wet and it was −30 degrees with wind-chill this morning so I helped her change into warmer pants and gave her a hand-me-down lavender sweater to wear over a t-shirt but she's never really worn a sweater because her arms are so long and she told me none of her friends have ever ever ever worn a sweater to school then completely embarrassed and humiliated she hid in the laundry room instead of eating the oatmeal in a jar
  which I made last night to speed up the morning.

My three-year-old didn't want to wear her unicorn dress after we already discussed wearing her unicorn dress she wanted to wear her Cinderella dress which is size 2T and she wears size 3T and also it has a brown stain from the kid who wore it for too many years before we got it then she wanted to wear her dress with black sparkle tights and not the white leggings that match and I decided not to care because she would need snow pants on top to avoid frostbite when we crossed the street and then three-year-old Cinderella told me she no longer liked oatmeal in a jar
  which I made last night to speed up the morning.

So I found a loaf of white bread in the freezer and jammed it apart with a butter knife and while the bread was toasting I went to look for my five-year-old's glasses which are supposed to be on the nightstand where they never are so I looked in the usual places like the bathroom her desk and the bottom of the dog's toy bin and couldn't find them so sent my husband a text to see if he knew where they were but he didn't and he was busy so I tried to talk my five-year-old out from under the folding table in the laundry room where she was crying on account of the lavender sweater she didn't want to wear and in response she announced she would not be wearing the sweater and I told her she would be cold because it was −30 degrees with wind-chill and she told me she didn't care because no kindergarten child in the history of kindergarten children at Scenic Acres School has ever ever ever ever worn a sweater to school and I said fine be cold before directing her to the oatmeal in a jar

which I made last night to speed up the morning.

Cinderella ate two bites of her toast and was looking for her clip-on rainbow dog while screaming and trying to pull another off her sister's bag but her own was actually at the bottom of the stairs where her sister threw it and I asked my five-year-old why she did that and where her glasses were but she didn't know so I asked where they were last and she couldn't remember then I said she would have to tell her teacher and she said I would have to tell the teacher because it was my responsibility then I tried to explain responsibility before giving my five-year-old her toothbrush and telling her she still had to brush even if she didn't eat the oatmeal in a jar

which I made last night to speed up the morning.

I checked the truck again for the glasses and couldn't find them then called the dog to come because she likes car rides and it was too cold for a walk and I lifted her into the truck because she's old and stiff and she smiled at me all ready to go and I went back in the house yelling for everyone to get their boots on and they did so I handed them their down coats and snow pants to carry since kids don't fit in car seats when they are bundled and my five-year-old started to cry because she was cold in the garage and I told her she could put on the sweater and she cried louder then Cinderella wanted her purple coat and I explained it was in the wash because she spilled an entire cup of milk on it yesterday and she would have to wear her pink coat that wasn't purple.

Then I carried my three-year-old under one arm and everything else under the other while calling for my five-year-old to get herself into the truck and I took one more run upstairs to look for the glasses which were on the nightstand but I didn't originally see them because the pink frames matched the cover of the *Pinkalicious* book they were on which reminded me that the daily library book was due back at school and I started flipping through the books on the nightstand looking for one that was not ours and couldn't find it so I wiped the glasses clean with my sweater and handed them to my five-year-old in the truck and she was mad because she was hoping the glasses were at the bottom of the dog toy bin.

I buckled her into her car seat and she started to cry again because the truck door was open and she was only wearing a t-shirt and then I closed the door and leaned against the truck thought about looking up school bus requirements even though we live half a kilometre from the school to see if she qualified but I knew she didn't and mostly I just wanted to enjoy the quiet for a minute but the screaming didn't stop so I drove toward our school but the Catholic school had already started and the parents were driving away and clogging up the roads so I drove slowly since the roads were dreadful.

I parked the truck across the street from the school where we are supposed to park as per the handout distributed on the first day of school registration and as per the weekly email even though there are only three other parents who actually park there and I unbuckled my five-year-old and told her to put on her jacket hat and mitts while I shoved the ladybug snack bag and the snow pants we didn't have time to put on into her backpack and double-checked for the rainbow dog and found the library book she was supposed to read last night before returning it the next day in her backpack but I couldn't remember if we read it and my five-year-old just sat in her car seat until I told her again to get out of her seat and put on the jacket hat and mitts or she would be really really really cold.

Then I got my three-year-old into her winter clothes which required discussing the pink coat that was not the purple coat and why we needed mitts and a hat and then I just put them on her and told my five-year-old to come out her sister's side of the truck since the roads were icy and I said she should climb out the sidewalk side anyway which made Cinderella mad because that was her door and so I explained it was not her door and then the dog tried to climb out hoping she was getting a walk but the dog had to wait in the truck because of the no-dog signs and because I was not hauling two kids and a dog across the street.

Cinderella was cold and angry and had a giant booger sitting on her lip like a little slug so I unlocked the door to get a Kleenex to wipe her nose and that made her angrier so I carried her screaming to the crosswalk because she refused to walk and the bell was going to ring and there was yelling when we got to the crosswalk and a firetruck full of six-foot-tall men who brave fires but not children stopped half a block back from the crosswalk because they saw me coming with one kid flailing around and another hanging onto my purse trying not to slip on the ice and it was probably hard for them to see through the exhaust fumes in the frozen air.

I was holding Cinderella sideways so she couldn't kick off her boots as we walked past a grandpa in the crosswalk who had already dropped his grandson at school and who I only see when everyone is screaming and I said good morning and carried my yelling three-year-old past the row of running cars parked in the school loop where they were not supposed to park past the red-faced parents watching my kid scream and set Cinderella down then I told her sister to walk ahead and she thought we should all walk together as if she was not in any sort of a rush and my three-year-old cried that she needed her own backpack even though she doesn't go to school and then another kindergarten mom whose daughter doesn't cry turned to look at us and she was wearing black heels with her pressed pants and I thought she's probably cold.

Then my five-year-old ran ahead to catch her friend and I remembered I didn't give her a hug so I called her back and kissed her pink cheek then gave her a squeeze and said I would be back in two hours and she hugged me through her giant puffy coat and then tried to run beside her friend in the heavy boots I made her wear while the principal held the door and I stood alongside the other mothers who were buried in snow gear and exhaust fumes.

And we sighed our shared relief for our children who made it to school before the bell rang and I think we were all grateful just to go home or on quiet commutes and not through the front doors to fill out Late Forms in the principal's office.

Finally, I carried my little Cinderella back to the truck and wondered how I could possibly fit my morning into those accusatory little boxes.

What reason could I ever give?

Travelling Light
Julianne Palumbo

From the window of our airplane
clouds stretch like sheets of bubble wrap
waiting to be popped.
I press my head against the tiny square and
imagine running across them.
My heels poke holes,
exposing pieces of blue.

Miles and minutes it all disappears,
puffs stretch to strands
dots to dashes
and I'm running away.

This a retreat from you
who drain the days from us:
fighting, feeding,
filling yourself on what's been missing.

And even as the fear of flying could ground us,
the fear of losing my life to your story
walks me down the tarmac.

One day my life was mine.
The next it was
tales of unknown horrors,
genetic wagers,
battles of a traumatized will.

I am safe here now
in the air
17,000 feet above you,
safe from your random turbulence,
your lurking currents,
your un-stowable baggage,
safe from what you might become.

Balloon Ride
Joan Crate

"G ET IN, BABE," you called, pulling up beside me in your beat-up Nissan. "I got you a birthday present."

Your crooked grin got me the way it always does, so even though I knew you were stoned, even though I was totally pissed about the way you had taken off on me and Maggie, I thought, *what the hell.* It *was* my birthday, and at that moment Mom was looking after Mags while I was supposed to be headed to McBride's for diapers. So I stood back while you climbed out the one working door of the car and let you nudge me across the driver's seat to the passenger's side.

"You ever going to fix the car door?" It was a rhetorical question. There was no way the car was worth fixing and even if it was, there was no way you would find either the money or the will to do it. "So where we going?"

You didn't answer, just put the pedal to the metal and we roared, muffler-free, along the highway. At Memorial Road you turned and I spotted a black pickup hitched to a small white trailer down by the cemetery.

At first I thought that truck belonged to Chad, the new youth pastor who everyone says still has a crush on me despite my fall from grace—a push my asshole brother Kevin says—but as we got closer, I saw that though it was the same make and probably even last year's model too, it was caked with dirt, the grill bug-splattered, and only two of the fluorescent orange hub caps were still attached. My Dad always faults Chad as *green around the gills*, but Mom says he's *a fine young man*, making her sound like a hundred years old when she's still young enough to turn into a lunatic every twenty-eight days. Whatever. But I knew Chad wouldn't let his ride look so shabby in a million years.

Then I noticed something else. On the ground in front of the truck was a mosaic. It was one of those hot air balloons, I realized, spread over the grass like a hallucination. As we parked, I studied it, a flaccid skin of tattoos much more colourful than any of yours, those buffalo skulls and wolf silhouettes that once drew me to you *like a moth to a flame*, as Kevin so poetically put it. Like Chad, Kev aspires to be a youth pastor, but he'll never be as chill in, like, *ever*. Chad had dazzled us all when he arrived from the city last year—all the girls, at least—with his buff bod, perfect teeth, and gleaming new truck.

After squeezing out the driver's door behind you and seeing the crazy grin on your face as you looked at the balloon, I started to fathom just what my birthday present was. "Oh, shit!"

I know I've told you I wanted to ride in a hot air balloon, but it was just a stupid fantasy, one I never thought could actually happen with my morbid fear of heights and your spectacular lack of cash. I told you the balloon story when what I really wanted was to rise above all the problems you got me into. Though it doesn't make any sense, I imagined us floating over this shithole town with its stampeding gossip, both of us and Maggie too, completely free. Untouched.

I watched you talking to the two guys holding the rim of the balloon. An old guy with faded tatts covering every centimetre of his stringy arms aimed a machine that shot a roaring flame into it. Before our eyes, the skin took shape.

"A magical flying machine," you said, laughing, making me laugh too even though I was trying to stay pissed at you.

We climbed into the basket, one of us on each side of our ancient *pilot*, as he called himself. I was so terrified, my heart practically leapt through my nursing bra. Even though it was a good two hours before I had to feed Mags, I could feel milk leak into my t-shirt.

As we rose, I clung to the handle attached to the side of the basket, my body a sack of panic. But you were thrilled, your head thrown back as you gazed up at the brightly patterned cloth pulling us up, your laughter tickling me with that old familiar sizzle, making me remember why I loved you. Love you.

As we got higher, I had to squeeze my eyes shut.

When I opened them again, I caught the blur of grass beneath us, the sky a singing blue, and to the west, mountains poking through like peaks of vanilla ice cream. I mean, as terrified as I was, this was way cool!

You reached over and grabbed my hand. "Holy shit," we shrieked together as we gazed away from our dreary little town with the big church, dingy houses, and beat-up farms, away from the other towns like ours—thirty, seventy, a hundred kilometres down the road—all with too much drought and hard-core religion. We threw our arms around each other, inseparable again. Looking in the other direction, we totally missed the storm cloud.

It engulfed us like a coma. Our pilot churned around us in a cyclone of activity, swearing, pulling ropes and switches, but the basket swung crazily in the wind.

You stumbled and I screamed. The wind shook us like a baby's rattle. I thought for sure we were going to crash. The rain pelted me into a corner and I had to shield my face, shivering and scared enough to pray.

After a while, the balloon went from near-horizontal to more vertical. It was still swinging from side to side, but not as wildly and I figured maybe we weren't going to drop out of the sky and splat conveniently on the cemetery grounds, after all. Gripping the rope, I managed to pull myself up and peer through the pelting rain for whatever corner you and the ancient mariner had crawled into. It was impossible to see clearly, so I called your name. I screamed it but the wind shoved the sound back down my throat. I fumbled with my non-gripping hand, trying to reach you. That's how I remember it: screaming, my hand groping, straining, touching nothing. The only sounds were howling wind and sluicing rain.

The sun was already sliding down the sky when I woke up, curled in the basket on the ground. The storm had vanished and the balloon skin was flattened on the grass, just as it had been when we first arrived. But your Nissan was nowhere to be seen. Neither was the black pickup with the white trailer. There were no balloon holders or tatted-up Jean-Luc Picard. No you.

I was cold as the gravestones huddled nearby, and I couldn't stop shivering. At least my milk had stopped leaking.

I climbed out of the basket and started walking to the highway. My phone still had a bit of juice, so I called Kevin. He didn't pick up. Didn't want to talk to me. Probably fed up with my *bad choices* like the rest of my family.

I'd have to hitchhike home, or at least to my parents' place, where I moved two weeks before when you left our little rental because you *couldn't hack the bullshit in this town anymore.* We had just finished lunch—the last of my aunt's perogies with sour cream too watery to sell—when you got the call from the plant. They were reducing hours and since you were low man on the totem pole—*no pun intended, ha-ha-ha*—you were cut to two days a week.

You grabbed a jacket and stormed through the door yelling you were going fishing with your brother for the weekend. Didn't even ask if it was okay with me. If I hadn't been so dazed, I would have wrestled you to the floor to keep you there, pinned you under me, if I could. I wasn't ready to be dumped again, first *because* of you, and now *by* you? But I just stood there, stunned. I mean, I had a baby to look after. We had a baby.

Trudging through the grass to the highway, I saw the sky had changed; no longer endlessly blue, no longer a black tantrum, but instead tattered like a billboard with most of the picture peeled away. Nothing was behind the remaining scraps of cloud, no colour, just blank space. Then the first bleed of sunset.

After four cars whizzed by, not even slowing, I called Dad. Unlike my asshole brother, he picked up.

Once I told him where I was, he hung up without another word. I didn't know if he was coming for me or not. But ten minutes later, he pulled up.

We didn't speak on the drive home. I sure didn't want to give him the opportunity to lecture me about taking off when the baby needed changing, how I had to *accept responsibility* and quit *taking advantage* of him and Mom. I sure couldn't take anymore of him being *disappointed* in my behaviour this past year, *not angry*.

But nothing, *nada*. Dad acted like everything was fine, just turned up the heat until I stopped shivering.

This much I know: you left me during a hot air balloon ride, the gift you gave me for my eighteenth birthday. But this time you left for good.

This doesn't make any sense, but now it seems like you were gone before you ever moved to our town, before we met at the Legion dance I went to with Becky when we told our parents we were babysitting for the *Marriage Repair* workshop at the church hall. You left before our long talks and giggles over root beer and fries at Bennie's, before making out in the Nissan, before I loved you. Our child, our little Maggie has never been born.

This is exactly what I wanted: to never have met you, to never have gotten pregnant, for you to never have started smoking up on a daily basis or get *downsized* from your job at the plant. I told you over and over: "I wish I never laid eyes on you!"

Now it's like I didn't.

Which is good, I mean, it really is, because without you, I am free as that stupid balloon sailing into a cleaned-up, stripped-down future. I don't have to endure the snub of the community's *upstanding citizens*, as you used to call them: my parents, brother, aunts, cousins, and uncles, even your parents, considered *not our kind of people* by my entire extended family, the whole ridiculously bigoted town. Without Maggie with her colic and rashes, life is so much simpler.

But I can't help it. I feel like I've had a major surgery, cut from breastbone to pubic bone with vital parts removed—my heart, child, and something else, like enthusiasm or maybe desire, a *joie de vivre*, as my French teacher used to say. What's left is an empty space. On weekends I wear maternity tops from the thrift store to cover it up.

Your whole life is before you, the school principal had the nerve to tell us last week at graduation, like she didn't know it was a moth-eaten cliché. *Graduates, each of you must ask yourself, what am I planning on doing with it?*

"I don't know," I whispered to Becky, my only real friend now you're gone. "I mean I just don't give a shit anymore."

Becs—still trying to convince her parents she should take drama in Red Deer rather than hairdressing in Stettler—rolled her eyes. "What's *your* problem? Marks decent enough to get into university if you want, a family that practically runs this town, and Pastor Chad making eyes at you every chance he gets: what more could *you* possibly want?"

"Yeah, well Chad's not the hottie he used to be," I countered, referring to the little pot where his six-pack used to be. What else could I say? I mean, how could Becky understand that a piece of my life got torn out and patched over. Everything that led up to me making the biggest mistake of my life, removed.

But I do want something. It's the answer to one simple question: Wherever you are—escaped from this town, the gossip, our *shame*, as my mother so eloquently put it, rejection and poverty—would you do it again?

I'm just wondering, because I would.

pritchard park

Katherena Vermette

she sits
on the far park bench
exhales cigarette smoke
and cold
her fingers trace
the rough
lines others have carved
into the wood

her youngest daughter calls
wants to swing
wants to be pushed
until her feet kick the sky
until her little face hurts
from wind
and laughter

she stubs out
her half-finished smoke
stumbles toward
the play structure

where her oldest daughter thumps
her boots across the frozen
play bridge
she likes the sound
how its hinges
have a special song
in winter

Memory Series #4
Marie-Manon Corbeil

The Mom Costume
Lisa Harris

I WAS SUPPOSED to be happy. My daughter was healthy *and*
beautiful. But there were downsides to birthing: exhaustion, pain,
disquietude. The tiredness and soreness would pass but I wasn't
sure about the unsettledness. It was as if I had pulled on this pudgy
postpartum flesh by mistake, a mom costume I tried on at the
Halloween store and the zipper had stuck while some other woman
walked off wearing my professional slacks.

It was as though my whole persona swooshed out of me with the
final push, bringing forth my daughter as well as a new identity, the
old one carted off in the tray with the placenta. People called me by a
new moniker: Mom. What had happened to Dr. Harris?

Working from home, I advised the Department of Defense: Army,
Navy, and Air Force on environmental regulations. This allowed me
the flexibility to take care of Lyda but complicated my identity crisis.
Who was I when I spoke to clients on the phone while nursing: a
consultant with secret clearance status or an in-over-my-head new
mom? My confusion grew when a colonel asked, "Is that a baby
in the background?" as if I had hoodwinked him, the outrageously
expensive advice given not by a professional but by a diaper changer.

To sort through my dilemma I joined a playgroup of women like
myself, women with careers: two engineers, a veterinarian, and a
marketing professional. At our first meeting I learned all had taken
lengthy maternity leaves. "I'm going back to work when my baby
starts school," Engineer One said. Engineer Two nodded. "I'm
planning to have another child and go back when *that* baby starts
kindergarten." Marketing Professional had quit her job. Veterinarian
filled in for other vets on vacation and had no intention of working
full-time. These women were not wrestling with identities. They
were moms.

I changed identities several times a day. Dressed in trousers and a
polo, I talked to officers while Lyda played on the other side of my
desk. Hanging up, I reclaimed mom clothes—shorts and a t-shirt.
Some client phone calls, which either engaged more of my skills
or were with high-up brass, required a different uniform: a silk

pinstripe jacket and navy-blue skirt. Somehow, the words that poured from my mouth while I wore a tank top didn't seem important. At the end of the day I determined who I had been by the laundry hamper's contents.

The playgroup moms wore shorts and t-shirts all day. They didn't talk about work or current events or housing prices. Or talk in acronyms. They discussed their babies' latest accomplishments or foibles. They talked bargain-hunting and Target deals.

"I bought five." Marketing Manager Leslie recounted how she had driven across town to snap up diapers at ten cents off a package.

"Call me next time," Veterinarian Mary Kay said.

"You don't think Josh'll grow out of the diapers before he uses them, do you?" Leslie added. "I had to get out of the house. I was going nuts."

Engineers One and Two did the math and nodded, as if to say, 'You bet it was a good deal. Wish I'd known.'

Every time I broached my wishy-washy identity, my conundrum was met with silence. By the time our children crawled, my friends had dropped their first names altogether and labelled themselves: Alex's Mom, Brian's Mom, Josh's Mom and McKinsey's Mom. I gave up correcting them when they called me Lyda's Mom, as they gave me a "what's your problem?" look.

My alias followed me to school—Lyda's teachers and friends called me Lyda's Mom. This etiquette snafu never would have occurred during my mother's era. Back then I would have been addressed as Mrs. Harris. No one would have thought of calling me by another name.

After the birth of my second daughter, I worried who I would be: Ava's Mom, Lyda's Mom, Dr. Harris, or simply me—and was "me" an amalgamation of all three?

I joined another playgroup, knowing Ava would benefit from interacting with peers. I lowered my expectations for identity-related discussions. Made sure I didn't slip into government-speak: "Developed an EIS for AFCEC with a FONSI within the POP," and resigned myself to listening to bargain-hunting stories.

During one meeting at a community pool, my cell phone rang: a contract officer from The Boeing Company (yes, that company). "Can I call you back?" I asked. He replied, "If you hang up I'm moving on to the next name on my list." No opportunity to change into my silk pinstripe, I had to wing it. Padding barefoot out of earshot of squealing kids, dressed in my Speedo two-piece, I discussed my bandwidth and how I could support Boeing's project.

Twenty minutes later I returned to the Jacuzzi having snagged a multi-year contract—in my mom costume. This time, without an inkling of inferiority, I felt my advice was worth the money I would charge. Soaking with the other moms—a pediatrician and a neurologist—I realized I no longer had to deny one persona for the other. I was both Mom and consultant. As we splashed with our toddlers, we called each other by the names printed on our graduate school diplomas: Nancy, Jane and Lisa, as well as Margaret's Mom, Voth's Mom and Ava's Mom.

SicknessSoftnessThunderJoy
Melanie Jones

1.

THIS SEASON changed us. Part of it was that you crossed over to two. (Everyone said the first year was the hardest and then they said the first two years were the hardest so I stopped believing that it would ever actually get easier and more spacious, but then you turned two and it did.) And part of it was that we moved away from Brooklyn and got three hours of our day back. Part of it was not having a car and needing to learn the skills of dressing for snowstorms and bikes, the skills of navigating all that. Of looking at the forecast to know when we might be able to make it to the grocery store. Part of it was the flu, and what happened afterward.

And for the record, it was the real flu, the influenza flu, not some cute sneezing and congestion for a few days. It was the knock-you-on-your-ass-weeping-because-your-spirit-has-broken, garbage-truck-parked-on-your-chest flu. That flu. I still haven't forgotten coming to your preschool at the beginning of December and seeing Lucy's deathly pale skin and staring red-rimmed eyes and thinking oh no, here it comes. (Lucicita. Why did no one scoop you up and take you home?)

I went down first. But I wasn't allowed just to be sick. I had to keep the show going. Three meals a day. On budget because we were so broke from the move. One night, it was my turn for bedtime, and I had been trying to get your dad to understand how tired I was. That this wasn't just a cold that the exhaustion was like stones in my cells or lead in the marrow and every movement or thought or effort was impossibly heavy. I'm lying in your bed trying to summon the energy to read you stories and he's doing chitchat, cheerfully off the parenting hook, and the rage and helplessness and cell-deep fatigue overflowed and I started sobbing
and I couldn't stop.
   "What's wrong?" he said.

"I'm sick! I'm sick! I'm fucking sick!" I wailed because I didn't have the energy or the language to say I needed help.

He stared at me. He said okay. Didn't offer to take over. Like in the algorithm of our shared-but-not-equal parenting, my turn for bedtime is simply my turn, no matter if I am flattened by viral load, in literal flames or being eaten alive by piranhas.

Please. Can you please take over? Why is that impossible to ask?

You went down next. Then your dad got it and you got worse instead of better. I stayed grounded through the biggest fever of your life, which was major for me. Thank God for best friends and text messages. For trusting the body. You were burning and you couldn't sleep and we lay there in the dark with rain sounds playing, staring into each other's eyes, blinking, and I said do you want some water and you whispered lie down and I said we need to find the old songs, the ancient songs and I felt more connected than I had in days and days, your eyes blinking and shining fever-bright in the dark.

2.

After a month of this, an entire month of dragging ourselves through every day, of being sick while caregiving, while parenting a toddler, your dad finally lost it. That morning, on the couch, he broke. Sat there sobbing with his sweatshirt draped over his head. Alone, with stones in his cells. We crawled beside him for a cuddle and some empathy, which was me teaching both you and him how to behave when someone needs support. I took you to school and came back.

"If you need NyQuil," I said, "I will go get it for you."

I talked to Auntie Jen on the way, I can't remember what about. We talked for at least twenty minutes while I stared at the 7-Eleven coolers wondering how it was possible there wasn't a single bottle of ginger ale in any of them.

I felt weirdly happy, almost giddy. Like your dad cracking open, like this trip to the gas station was a door unlocking and I was finally emerging into the thin, dry sunlight after a month trapped in 800 square feet of sickness.

On my knees for weeks, but only just reaching surrender. Only just, after two-ish years of motherhood, finding the sweet softness of Rumi's chickpea beaten against the side of the pot.

Finally, the freedom that was letting go of all those not-mine expectations, all those timelines, all those outcomes. I was weak. I was skinny. Pale and full of snot. Boiled and beaten, finally soft, frantically grateful. How long I hoped for softness. How hard I struggled and thrashed.

How effortless, then, to soften, sudden, walking home from 7-Eleven in the sunshine carrying several pounds of desperation NyQuil, and lemon iced tea, listening to our Jose Gonzalez breastfeeding song from when I was a newborn mother wailing, cold and scared, unable to see colour.

3.

I want you to know that the first two years of your life were filled with love, but also rage. I have been so unbelievably angry. I'll explain it to you someday, probably, but my rage scared me. It felt uncontrollable. Like it would take me over. Like it would tear down everything I had been trying so hard to build for you and with you.

There's a reason I breastfed you so long. Why you've slept with me every night since you were born. Why you will never know what a time out is. I just thought there would be more support.

I thought there would be all this help and there wasn't. It was just me. Mark. The books. The sketched outlines of a village sitting in my cell phone contacts, dormant and still, while I walked alone in the flat gray Brooklyn winter, trying to fill the hours.

And yes, parenting got more spacious when you turned two, but then it compressed in a new way. Because you found your own rage. How was I supposed to guide you through yours when I couldn't manage mine?

Mothering myself at age forty-two. Raw and vulnerable and without skin. Reaching toward healing like a collapsing star. Trying to make sense of the tasks of the day: chop wood, carry water, feed my people, be present to your shining. And if I couldn't make sense of it, to let that be okay. There was a part of healing that required me to disintegrate. Which sounds Not Good, but it was disintegration down to the elements, even the minerals breaking apart under the frozen earth, so I only took what was needed for the next part. Falling apart as a requirement for coming together, or at least for coming home to my self and my cells.

Disintegration as integration.

Doing things differently. Moving away from the habitual and the holding. Opening and softening and collapsing into the cold ground. Trusting that she'll hold me firmly. I've got you. I've got you.

I practised staying connected to the heart. I practised stopping when I felt angry. Stopping to calm down, not harden or stew. My whole being was focused: stayed connected. I became skilled at and surprisingly passionate about midwifing your tantrums. People often smirk at the word tantrum. But toddler thunder is no joke. It is sacred work. It's deep work. For the parent and the child. I am, right now, teaching a human how to engage with big emotion.

I wasn't particularly well trained in this regard. Big emotion was not okay. My feelings were ignored or diverted. I was instructed by people I trusted not to feel them. And like caregiving while sick, I had to parent myself while parenting you.

You brought your thunder to our neighbour's house one afternoon. Our neighbour didn't know what to do. She tried to distract you. I know this was an effort to support us, but we didn't need help. You were letting your feelings rip like a champion and I was making sure you felt supported and loved as you did. I protected your head from coffee table corners while you thrashed. I laid on top of you, one of your favourite ways to feel safe. I held you and told you I loved you and I was there for all of the big mad and big sad you were feeling.

There was a moment when I realized my tantrum parenting had an audience for the first time. A moment when I wondered what it looked like from the outside. Whether I should change something about what I was doing because I was being watched. Is it weird that I'm lying on my child, pressing her arms firmly into an acquaintance's couch, murmuring mama's here, mama's here?

I took a deep breath. And I decided that it serves no one to hide the reality of big, deep work. It serves no one for me to hide my labour or yours. Becoming a human is major. It's important. It's holy and it's fucking messy. It's learning how to be with ourselves, which is foundational to being with each other.

Lying with you that night, you crawled on top of me and stroked my face in the darkness. "I'm here," you whispered. "I'm here."

4.

During those hard few months, we began this daily healing practice of over-the-top lip synch to "Let It Go." We played it on repeat at full volume morning and night, dancing and often, in my case, crying. (I'll rise like the break of dawn, damn it.) And once you learned the words, you sang. Loudly.

You ran back and forth along the long line of beat-up hardwood between the front door and the kitchen, yelling, "Let it go! Let it go! Let it go!"

Then, suddenly, you dove onto your pile of library books. You demanded the library card and scanned it under the side table. "Boop." Then you scanned all your books, the entire Halloween section, who cares it was February. "Boop. Boop. Boop. Boop." You wanted to dance on the trail of books you left on the floor and I said something about needing to respect the books. But watching you, I wasn't convinced that books aren't made for dancing on.

Boop.

Your delight is this open-mouth lit-up thing. God, I want you to keep this delight. Your joy makes my joy feel so possible. It shows me the sky-high ceiling for what's available to me if I just cut the dark and twisty shit. And I don't mean that in a self-flagellating way, but in the way that you can flip from growling at me and stomping into the corner to suddenly pointing and grinning, triumphantly yelling, "M for Maelle!" In the way that you bring your whole self to everything you do and feel and say.

I want to bring my whole self. Not anchored down by "yeah but." Fully alive. Your joy is just that: your joy. I'd eat it with a spoon, but it belongs to you. I have to get my own. I need to practise.

I'm already practising. Gesturing wildly, eyebrows knitted together with intensity: here I stand in the light of day. My joy is not a holy grail I have to toil through scary forests and rocky crags to find. And it's not joy in a bubble, either. It's joy under fire. Joy in a body that's been sick for three months. Joy on too little sleep. Joy, regardless of condition. I can just start with guilty pleasure Disney songs and almost-dried-up markers and work my way up up up until the moment when my feet hit the floor in the morning even if I'm tired and surly with pink eye and sore throat I can say thank you thank you and mostly mean it and know that we have everything we need to connect with the old songs, the mother, the river that runs through us all the time whispering in the darkness I've got you baby I've got you I'm here.

The Stand of Flamingos
Elaine Hayes

Jenna charged the exit door and resisted the urge to glance back at the security guard escorting her. Once outside, she hurried through a fog of exhaled nicotine, but she withheld the exaggerated coughs she normally directed at the smokers, smokers who still had jobs but who huddled around a concrete waste bin like the homeless around a bonfire. As she rushed to catch the crosswalk's green light, the contents of her Bankers Box shifted, and her shouldered tote slid and pinched her wrist. She ignored the discomfort and strode straight ahead as though she had purpose, a destination.

Three blocks later, Jenna entered the ladies' room at the mall. She sat on a toilet and sorted through the contents of the box. Stale snacks. Pens. Tattered loafers she'd kept under her desk for fire drills and power failures, times when she'd be forced to climb down fifteen flights of stairs. A mug that the girls—Bella, age eight, and Mallory, age five—had given to her for Mother's Day, and, at the bottom of the box, a framed photo of her smiling family on a long-ago beach.

Jenna placed the photo in the envelope with the letter outlining the benefits to which she'd be entitled. Three months of severance. Employment search assistance. Counselling.

When Dean had received his layoff notice, sixteen months earlier, he'd driven home before calling Jenna. Their home number had appeared on her cell phone, and she'd panicked because no one should've been at home midday. She envisioned an emergency at the girls' school or daycare, one in which there hadn't been time to contact parents. A bomb scare. A shooting, maybe.

"They let me go," Dean said, breathless, his words tripping over themselves. "The branches are consolidating but they paid me a decent severance, so we'll be okay for a few months and then I can collect Employment Insurance."

Dean had been right. They'd been okay. They'd eliminated vacations and restaurant meals and they hadn't renewed the lease on Jenna's car; she took the bus downtown on weekdays, so they decided they could share Dean's, and he'd pick her up each day at the end of the route. They vowed, though, to maintain home life for the girls as normal as possible, and they used their savings for the girls' activities. They hadn't yet touched the education funds, but now they had only two months of Dean's Employment Insurance left.

Jenna's eyes stung as she thought back to how she'd muttered support but had silently blamed Dean. Why had he been the first laid off at his branch? Why had he so often volunteered to work from home when Bella was sick and then boast about playing video games all day? And how often had he called, late-afternoon, explaining that he was still out for lunch with clients and wouldn't have an appetite for dinner? Jenna couldn't help thinking, back then, that maybe he'd still have had a job if he'd been more dedicated, more responsible, more like her.

Now, though, as she sat on a public toilet with the remains of her own job not even filling half the cardboard box, her smugness embarrassed her. She slipped on her loafers and jammed her pumps, the mug and the envelope into her tote. She abandoned the box on a wet countertop.

The bus was sparsely occupied, but it was still overheated and reeked from the morning's rush hour. Hairspray and garlic, sweat and overripe fruit. She sat at the back and dug through her bag for her cellphone, but, remembering she'd surrendered it alongside her office key-card, withdrew her sunglasses instead, as though embarrassed to be caught looking for what no longer existed.

The bus exited the downtown core, meandered along Memorial Drive, and stopped at the Calgary Zoo, a stop not serviced in her normal rush-hour commute. Several passengers disembarked, and, on impulse, Jenna joined them. She needed a payphone, and she needed air, too. A quick walk would clear her head, she reasoned, and would give her time to compose both herself and her explanation to Dean. Besides, he wasn't expecting to pick her up for several hours.

Jenna enquired about a payphone as she flashed her zoo pass. The pass was an annual family membership Jenna's mother had given to the family for Christmas; the gift had made sense, given Dean's layoff and their anticipation of another summer vacation at home. The ticket agent directed Jenna to the far end of the zoo, to a concession stand area near the Kids Zone.

Jenna strode past the penguins and concrete dinosaurs and crossed the pedestrian bridge over the Bow River. Since the flooding a few years earlier, several more of the zoo's cages had been upgraded to chain-link enclosures, which gave the impression of larger, less confining spaces for the animals. She dodged the free-roaming peacocks, passed the still-vacant elephant enclosure, but paused briefly at the flamingos, who appeared agitated. The birds not holding their heads underwater honked and grunted and stretched their necks and tossed their heads in an odd display of synchronicity. *The word flamingo*, stated a sign, *is derived from the Latin word flamenco, or fire. They may appear to be clumsy flyers, but these birds are powerful and capable of reaching speeds of 55 kilometres per hour.*

They stood in a foul-smelling pond, and a low fence, constructed of ropes strung through wooden posts, bordered their area. Jenna noted that the fence was a primitive version of the stanchions and velour belts she'd once ordered to manage line-ups for a show home opening.

She berated herself for not anticipating the layoff. As Project Scheduler for a custom home builder, she'd foolishly credited the improved performance of plumbers and framers and roofers to the relationships she'd diligently cultivated. She realized now, though, that it had been an early sign that the housing market was still not recovering, and that it was, instead, coming to a standstill.

She couldn't find a payphone in the concession stand area, and, since the kiosks hadn't yet opened, there were no employees to ask for help. She returned to the flamingos, sat on a bench upwind from them, and waited. She had no idea of the time. But there was nothing else to do until she could find a phone to call Dean. She rehearsed the announcement of the layoff. Every effort sounded flat and desperate, even though she knew he'd respond with sympathy, with reassurances, with unconditional support. He'd blame the economy and the price of oil—"it's feast or famine in this city"—and wouldn't mention how she'd blindly boasted about her scheduling prowess and the potential for advancement in the company. He'd probably suggest that they splurge on pizza for dinner, too, because she'd had such a rough day.

Jenna also knew that, through all this, she would be alert for hints of blame. She'd analyze every pause, every change in pitch, every syllable, every corner of his speech.

Female and male flamingos are identical, said another sign. *They both sit on eggs and feed their chicks.*

Jenna realized she'd forgotten to grab her lunch from the office fridge. Dean had packed it, ensuring, as always, that she never had the same salad and sandwich combination twice in one week. She regretted now that her overall behaviour toward Dean's tireless work at home also hadn't been supportive. In the evenings, she'd barely feigned interest as he shared the minutiae of his day. He folded towels hot from the dryer, and not one would ever tumble to the floor from a crammed linen closet shelf. He sourced the perfect paint for Bella's perfect science project. He organized the flotsam and jetsam of two young girls, and no one ever wasted time hunting for a headband or a sharpened pencil.

Jenna wondered how Dean hadn't drowned in the drudgery, as she had, how his work at home hadn't left him at the end of each day with a dull loathing for morning.

Five months into her first maternity leave, she'd floated the idea of her early return to work. Dean had laughed. "Don't be silly. We're managing just fine," he said. "What's for dinner?"

Jenna's mother recommended more sunlight and antidepressants and pointed out that Bella was a good baby, one who ate, shit and slept well. "And why, dear God, do you want to return to clerical work?" her mother said.

Jenna ignored the insult that her job arranging trades and inspections and lumber deliveries was not an essential service like her mother's nursing job had been, like her father's police work had been. No one died if Jenna ordered the wrong kitchen sink.

She wanted to respond that she didn't care how insignificant her job was, but she said nothing more to her mother, and nothing more to Dean. She didn't mention her idea to her sister Maureen; Maureen had three children in preschool and never intended to return to work. She didn't dare talk to her best friend Linda; after multiple miscarriages, Linda and her partner were considering adoption. How could she admit to these women, women who were clearly more loving, more motherly than she, that her days at home were destroying her? What words could she use that didn't make her sound like a monster?

Jenna stayed home for the entire benefit periods with Bella and then Mallory. At naptime, Jenna stroked her infant's wispy hair and kissed her fingertips and asked herself why she didn't love her baby enough to want to spend every minute with her. *What's wrong with me?* she wondered. Why couldn't she be like other women?

Jenna rose from the zoo bench and viewed the menu at the first open kiosk and cringed at the prices. She cursed herself for leaving her stale snacks, left over from what she so easily and casually referred to as "a seminar," behind in the Bankers Box. She asked for the time and the location of the nearest payphone and ordered only an iced coffee. Back at the bench, she removed her blazer. She was warm, but she also felt conspicuous, as though her business suit broadcasted the fact she should be at work, that she should be productive rather than whiling away time, alone at the zoo.

Their vibrant colours are produced by their food source, and they are pale in captivity unless their diet is sufficiently supplemented.

During her maternity leaves, Jenna spent time every week with Maureen, who was selling candles and Tupperware in the evenings. To escape the boredom, Jenna also tried dabbling in ceramics and yoga and meditation. At the end of each day, though, as she plugged in her lavender-oil diffuser, she wondered why everyone—Dean, her family, her self-help books—counselled that a healthy, balanced disposition could be achieved and sustained with outside activities, as long as those activities didn't involve paid employment. She recognized her own cowardice, her inability to reject everyone's expectations and return to work early. But she couldn't bear the shame of her own failures.

While on leave with newborn Mallory, though, she vowed she'd never be in that stuck-at-home situation again. She decided that, once back at work, she'd invent a business trip or, better yet, a training seminar. She'd visit a private clinic across the border. She'd use her own credit card, rather than their joint card, to finance the visit, and she'd withdraw a little money from the girls' education account, if complications arose post-procedure.

There are many terms for a group of flamingos: a flamboyance, a colony, a flock and a stand. These groups are their main defence against predators.

Preschoolers, tethered together by a skipping rope, balked at the smell of the flamingos' fetid pond, and, as they were quickly whisked away, Jenna thought back to her family's last vacation. The week's highlights had included a visit to the zoo and a public pool, followed by dinnertime picnics in the back yard. Over that two-week period, without realizing what was happening, Jenna slipped into the role as cook, cleaner, disciplinarian, roles that hadn't been so obvious when they'd travelled on real vacations. Mealtimes became charged with disagreements and complaints. The living room carpet was an obstacle course of dolls and stickers and crushed crayons. Laundry mildewed in the washer. Without warning, her own meagre plans for a book or a quiet cup of tea evaporated. She longed for a soft cry in the tub.

Jenna sipped her kiosk coffee and studied the label on the cup as though the solution to its bitterness could be found there. She thought of her maternity leave days and how, at breakfast, she'd read the sides of cereal boxes so often she could still cite the nutritional facts of every Cheerios variety.

Scientists don't know why flamingos stand for hours on one leg.
The sign looked a little less weathered than the others. Maybe, Jenna thought, in response to relentless questioning from zoo-goers, staff had decided it was best to admit their ignorance, their inadequacies.

The wind shifted. Jenna thought of the decorative flamingo designs that were now gracing the covers of home decorating magazines, displacing the trends of owls and octopuses, and wondered if those trendsetters had ever spent time studying live creatures.

There are more plastic flamingos in North America than real ones, said the last sign.

Jenna tugged at the passenger door handle. It was locked.
Dean fumbled with the buttons on the driver's door, and she climbed in and tossed her tote bag on the floor of the back seat, as always, below Mallory's happy, dangling legs.

"So?" Dean shifted, shoulder checked. "How was your day?"
Before Jenna could answer, Mallory announced: "I got new ballet slippers today! And guess how high I can count? A billion!"

"Don't be stupid," said Bella.

"Ow!"

Dean glanced at Jenna, shoulder checked again, and merged into traffic.

She did not turn to lecture Bella and Mallory, nor did she threaten them with a time out. Instead, Jenna slid her feet out of her pumps, as she always did for the ride home, and stared straight ahead.

"I lost my cellphone today." She paused. Swallowed. "I'll get a new one tomorrow. It'll be a new number, though." She shrugged, even though Dean's gaze was focused ahead. "For security reasons."

She patted her blazer pocket and felt the resistance, the reassurance of the zoo's annual pass inside.

Date Night

Kyle Nylund

Bana Thighearna nan Eilean[1]
(Our Lady of the Isles)
Anne Sorbie

Why are statues of the Holy Mother
pale blue   and white
subtly shiny   halo-ed   hallowed
even plaster-cast

Her hands in that annoying open gesture
as if to say   the whole world
no   universe
is welcome to come close and suckle her tapered tits

Why do some include the child
as if the woman
hymen intact
doesn't have enough to bear already

The child appears   sometimes
on her lap   in her arms
perched on her shoulder
or incredibly even standing on her hands
elevated

His head above hers
His hand on her head   benevolent
as he is in Our Lady of the Isles

installed high on Ruabhal[2]
on South Uist   ironic

---

[1] Our Lady of the Isles is a sculpture of the Madonna and Child, on South Uist in the Outer Hebrides of Scotland.

[2] The statue is situated on the western slopes of Ruabhal, a hill near the northern end of South Uist.

There she looks north
waiting   wanting the wind

as if called upon in effigy
as if to mother the place
in quiet protest
daring us to defy her
protection   as if her figure provides
a luscious lick on the land

Granite Mary hoisting her generous son
is an instrument of conjecture

Mary was used
to resist
as mothers often are
as archetypes of defence
convenience
succour and strength
as an homage
or a giant swollen edifice
to be pricked

What did you think?

To be taken for mothering
requires that the arms are ever open
that the palms
or the rest of the body for that matter
are permanently on call
Listen

The proof is in another statue
here
near the door
to the Church of Conjecture

On the outside
Mary is renewed
recast in plaster
as white as Paris

Inside steel rods
concealed in her empty arms
fling them to the same height
as the grown child's on the cross

The halo perches
on another that rises
from the back of her neck

We only see the tip of that rod

The rest is buried
iceberg deep in her spine
unstable now
after the brute force   upon entering
sheared off the holy wings
of the vertebrae
in a circumcision of laminae
Her bare toes curled
and gripping in pain

The serpent's head bulging
under her right foot

Edges of gold sandals shining
at the hem of her dress

The same leaf   mirrored
on the rosary that
corsets her waist   thin
as it was before the burden of the child

The gilded beads' first decade and cross
pointing lazily
to that deep valley
yes that one
the one that all men
say they love best

The statue of Mary here presented
is glamorous and calling

Defined by Hollywood hair
bobbed and blonde

As if the Madonna
made over as a Marilyn

perpetuates the mystery
of pointed mammary

Great and white
and dripping   always
always   from the sky

Blood Count
Susan Ouriou

at the lab
they poke and they prod
some gentle some not
exclaim at the crease in my arm
its absence of veins
like the back of my hand
not knowing
i bled with my child

i have a question
never answered
one i ask more and more
why is it so
in the grand scheme of things
that a child
has got to bleed

for the blood
tests
for the blood
lets
for the blood
count
always off

a daughter
my child

they can poke
they can prod
try my left
then my right
start over again and again
my body has spoken quite clearly
the giving must come to an end

Here and There, Everywhere in Between
Kelly S. Thompson

I SIT DRY-EYED at the doctor's office when she diagnoses me with Polycystic Ovarian Syndrome, or PCOS, not at all shocked. Essentially, I'd already diagnosed myself online, something I rarely do because in our family, considering our histories, it's easy to slip down the slope of medical terror. Besides, I've had worse.

"You know, the name is actually a misnomer. Many PCOS patients don't often have cystic ovaries," the doctor says as she punches letters into her keyboard, not looking at me. "It's often the other symptoms; weight gain, hirsutism, acne. You know, the hormonal stuff."

"Wonderful. Fatness with chin hair and backne. At least I could hide lumpy ovaries." I look into my lap, where my stupid, cystic ovaries and coordinating barren womb taunt me like bullies. "This is ironic timing, though."

"Oh?" The doctor continues to type, making out referral paperwork.

"My sister had her second child yesterday."

The doctor conveys the appropriate amount of support for my plight, combined with elation for my new niece; a premature five-pound dumpling now sitting under a UV light. "So, back to your health." PCOS is a result of my body making too much testosterone, she tells me. Says I need to focus on maintaining my current healthy weight, although that will be a challenge considering my system will now cling to fat in a death match with my metabolism. Taking birth control will help with the acne and hair, she says. The irony is not lost on us. "Most people with PCOS struggle to conceive, but that doesn't mean it's impossible with fertility treatment. So maybe touch base once we get you into the OB. Okay?"

"So, I'd have to screw with my hormones, that are already screwed, to have children."

The doctor is sympathetic, eyebrows arching into a compassionate steeple. "Well, you also have several autoimmune disorders. Former radiation on your thyroid. You know, these things all add up. Medical intervention doesn't have to be a bad thing in terms of birthing a child."

"I guess I just worry that…" I think of Joe and the fact that he is five years older than me, nearly forty, always having wanted children. I think of the way little ones gravitate towards him, engage in fake sword battles or request stories read, *pretty please, one more time.* I think of our shared fantasy—of a boy named Huck or a girl named Gwen, *just one,* we'd agreed while sipping wine and dreaming during date night, *no more than one*—slipping away. I think of the fact that my family used to joke that I would beat my own children out of frustration, because *Kelly has no patience! ha ha!* And how I would laugh along with them, knowing I didn't want kids then or ever, until I met the man who was like a walking advertisement for the perfect dad. I think of how that very joke has given the finger to karma and resulted in a now permanently childless me. "…that messing with hormone balance could make me a ranging psychopath that no one would actually want to have children with."

"Listen, you won't know until we investigate some more, right?"

I nod wordlessly, am still nodding as I get into my car, start the ignition and blare heat onto my cupped hands in the tart April air. My car is loaded to the hilt because I'm uncertain of how long I'll be gone.

I turn on a podcast, ignorant of its contents. I have to hurry to Toronto's Mount Sinai Hospital. Break speed limits. Wish I could teleport. Because it was this one pesky appointment that kept me from leaving yesterday, when my sister Meghan was induced and gave birth to my niece, just as she was promptly diagnosed with stage four sarcoma soft tissue cancer, muttering the news to me over the phone like a drunken teen, high on painkillers because the tumour burst.

I don't cry the whole way there. No point in crying over all the household milk that will never spill in the hands of my own pudgy toddler.

Meghan closes her eyes as the chemo drips in. I hold her hand, hold my nose, hold my breath, trying to avoid being a writer and observer in this cancer centre. I want nothing but to forget this room—its sparkling floors, its bathroom designated for patients only (radiation warnings!), its stainless-steel blanket warmer for heating bony legs.

"God, I'm exhausted," she says. "Parenting with cancer is a bitch."

"You're such a whiner. At least you delivered nice and premature so your vagina made it out relatively unscathed." Meghan laughs at my bad joke, always does. Yet her smile fades into the greyish pillow, which is thready from overbleaching. "Mothers of those eleven-pounders wish they were you."

She chuckles. "Easy for you to say. You try having kids. It's exhausting." Then she smacks herself on the forehead. "God, sorry. I forgot."

"You forgot my barren uterus while receiving chemo?" I clutch a hand to my chest like a dramatic opera singer. "How dare you!"

"Can I blame the cancer?"

"You can blame that shit for everything." I take her hand and give it a squeeze.

"Seriously though. I mean, not all motherhood involves the traditional give birth kind, right?"

"Guess not. Besides, if I had kids, I'd probably forget them in the back seat when grocery shopping, then find cops tapping their toes outside of my Town and Country van."

"You said you'd die before driving a minivan."

I'd always been unabashed about not wanting kids, proud of bucking trend when my high school friends already had broods by their mid-twenties. I would watch whatever I wanted on television, I said. Eat all the chocolate. Snooze in the middle of the afternoon. Mine would be a life of leisure. I told myself all of these things. "Well, at least we know *you* will definitely die before you drive a minivan."

Meghan laughs so hard at this that she starts coughing, her face gone red. When we were kids, she nursed dolls, made them sandwiches and one for me, read me bedtime stories, and then later, as a teen and into adulthood, approached every male interaction for a way to create that love. I watched from the sidelines, internally mocking her lame hopes. *Motherhood. Ugh. What a low bar to set.* How had I ignored that the bars were self-arranged and self-sabotaged? "I love the shit out of you, Kell." Her eyes go glassy, emotive. "You know that, right?"

"I know, Meg."

She will keep telling me, worried for all the moments where we never said the words aloud.

"She's such an attention whore, am I right, ladies?" Meghan laughs with the nurse, as hard as she can considering the morphine, the tumour like a tire around her waist, the fact that she doesn't have the energy to hold her own glass of water. The nurses have slotted into our macabre sense of sisterly humour like well-fitting gloves. "There goes my sister and her 'cancer.' Making it all about her." I flick mocking air quotes as the nurse fiddles with the morphine pump settings.

"Everything in the world is all about me," Meghan croaks. I bring a glass to her lips, wiggle the straw until it meets her lips. With my sleeve, I dab at a dribble of spit that is working its way down her semi-open mouth.

"Don't we know it, lady!" The nurse gives Meghan's foot a gentle swat. "Then again, as our longest lasting resident, you get all the extra attention you want." Eight weeks we've been sitting in this hospice—with its long hall, thrumming air-conditioning and antiseptic-scented bathrooms—for longer than we hoped, because hope has no place here, really, other than hope for lack of pain or an easier death. Other "residents" come and go, literally, within days. But Meghan is young. Her heart, at least, is healthy, and this keeps her going even when we dream—out of compassion, selfishness, exhaustion—that it will stop.

"That's me," Meghan says, wincing in pain as she adjusts herself in bed. "Always knew I'd break some kind of record."

"And longest-lasting hospice resident is the one you want to set? Lofty goals, Meg."

"Well, you've been here every day too," the nurse says. "You two are like our little sister warriors." She leaves with promises to return with a new fentanyl patch.

"She's right," Meghan says once she's gone. "You've been here all summer. You should go home. Enjoy time with Joe. Pot Roast, too."

I crawl next to her in bed, inching myself between the metal hospital railing and her thin body. We've always been a bit fat, Meghan and I, in a curvy way I've enjoyed. I barely recognize her now, her arms like the desiccated duck wings I feed to my dog. "Meg, wherever you are, that's where I am. Okay?" We lace fingers and I give her a kiss on the palm, careful to avoid her IV. She nods but says nothing else, tears slipping into her pyjamas.

"Thanks for looking after me." Tears fall in earnest now, but I pretend not to notice. We will both be undone if I do.

"What are sisters for if not to, literally, wipe your ass?"

"Parents. Parents wipe asses." She holds her palm in the air, miming the action like she is changing a diaper mid-air, imaginary wipe at the ready.

"Ah, well there goes my dreams of dodging the mom bullet, eh?"

"What can I say? I live to make your dreams come true." She smiles weakly and I want to take a photo, capture her like a firefly in a jar.

"Oh yeah. That's us. Living the dream. Alright, stop being so lazy. Let's get you in the shower, eh? You stink." I hold my nose for comedic effect.

"Do I?" She sniffs a pit in response, her body moving in slow motion.

"Of course not." If she knows I'm lying, she doesn't say. My sister smells of rot, likely because her coccyx is exposed, gangrenous around the edges, with the rest of her covered in a scaly rash, weeping bedsores. She's oozing disease, seeping it from her pores. If I think hard enough, I can still picture in this new body's place plump cheeks and dimpled thighs, just like mine. "But it'll make you feel better."

She acquiesces and lifts up her arms like a child reaching for its mother. I scoop her slight frame into my arms and carry her like a princess to the shower, where I place her in the waiting seat. Then I stand in my bra and underwear and gently glide a washcloth across her fragile skin, frothing it with all-natural soap because, I rationalized in the store, it was healthier. Meghan leans into the spray and closes her eyes. I wonder if she too dreams of soft curves bared to the water.

I check the rear-view mirror obsessively, looking for signs that I've not buckled my niece and nephew's car seats properly. I googled the procedure before I left the house, watched a few YouTube videos, but I'm still uncertain. All of this—the diaper bag, the mini monkey-printed mittens, the plasticky buckles of their winter coats—feels uncertain.

"Who wants to sing a song?" I ask, my voice high and tight. The kids appear ready. My parents and I, however, are nervous, simultaneously craving time with the children and yet barely able to stand it—these walking, talking, Meghan look-alikes that are not her, can never be her, and yet are her all at once. "Hello back there?" In the mirror, I see Lily smile gummy and wide, but still no words for me. Is she even speaking yet? When are kids old enough to talk? Sammy is staring out the window pensively. "No one wants to sing for Auntie?"

"Auntie," Sammy says, his voice serious. But he does not make eye contact. "My mommy is in heaven." He is all matter-of-fact, emotionless. A typical four-year-old comprehension of death.

I swallow hard, keep my eyes on the lane in front of me. The yellow line warbles like a mirage. "I know, Piggie. We miss Mommy, don't we?"

"She's an angel now."

"Yes." The word squeaks from my lips as a few tears do, too. I swipe at my face, annoyed. *Keep your shit together, Kelly.* "You know, buddy, your mommy was Auntie's sister. Just like Lily is your sister."

"You have a sister?" He's interested now, leaning forward against the confines of his booster seat. He smiles at this idea of me having a sibling, his eyes full of wonder as though he can't imagine someone as old as me with a mini relation in tow. His eyes are the same colour as Meghan's. As mine.

"That's right. Auntie's sister was your mommy."

"I'm sorry your sister died, Auntie." And then, like a Disney movie playing on the rear-view mirror, he reaches across the expanse of my father's Lincoln and takes his sister's mittened hand.

I pull over to the shoulder, the tires skidding against gravel. I can barely breathe, my throat tight, my hands shaking. And it's cold. Or hot. Maybe both. Sun glares off the snow, cascading around the interior. Where are my sunglasses? What time is it?

"Are we at Grandpa's now, Auntie?"

I turn to face Sammy, his eyes bright. "Almost, buddy. We're almost there."

When we get to my mom and dad's house, Sammy and Lily launch into their arms. They do not play strange with us. They do not cry or complain. They do not get upset about being in the home they have only ever visited with their mother. Instead, we complete puzzles, play hide and go seek, colour outside the lines.

I help Lily balance a tall wooden block on top of another. When the tower reaches her desired height, she topples it over and we laugh together as I poke her round toddler belly. Then, as though a switch has flipped, she pushes hair from her face like a woman on a mission, toddling over to the entertainment cabinet where a photo of Meghan sits. It's a family snapshot favourite, and her hair is chocolatey like our mother's but curled and shoulder-length. Her cheeks are rosy and plump and freckles spray across her nose and cheeks. She is my opposite, to look at.

"Mama." Lily takes the photo from the cabinet and presses it to her chest. "Mama." She holds the frame in the air now, triumphant. Mom, Dad and I watch like movie characters, our eyes welled, hands wrought.

"That's right, sweetie," I say, the only one capable of speaking. "That's Mommy."

She waddles to my side, having spent most of the day glued to me, a little human Velcro piece. "Mama?" She holds the photo to me as if asking a question. *You? Mommy?* No, no that can't be it because Meghan and I look nothing alike, right? Yet I sound like my sister, maybe smell like our shared childhood and whispered secrets. Perhaps these are tangible qualities to be sensed by those unjaded by loss.

I pull my niece into my arms and snuggle her downy hair. I don't correct her. Don't offer her an answer to the question she did not ask. We are content for the day to let the words remain unsaid, unknown, comforted that there is a Mommy, somewhere, and she is here and there and everywhere in between.

Crohn's
Liz Kingsley

My thirteen-year-old son is shrinking. At his worst, he can't sit
upright or climb stairs; lying on his side is the only position that
doesn't hurt. When the pain is most acute, he kneels naked on the
carpet, his butt pointed up toward a fan blowing cold air on his
anus. Hoping my maternal breath will bring relief, I blow on it
too. He was an infant the last time I was this close to this part of
him. I massage his thighs, calves, and arms until he asks me to stop.
What was once his adorable anus is now the sign of the guerrilla
warfare that his immune system is waging on itself, chronic illness.
I move the fan in closer, blow harder, trying to send the disease into
oblivion, powerless.

Thoughts 6
Doris Charest

Full-Body Tattoo
Dorothy Bentley

They unfurl for you, from foetal to free.
Stars form as needles pierce
rainbow hues. What images will
you surface? Apothecary pin-prick
muscle memories of
trauma and thrills;
metaphoric torso dioramas spread
thigh flowers trailing-trellis back to
shoulders—disguised visions and
dreams of babies—
swollen womb and throbbing breasts.

Missing: accumulated deaths.

Skin tinglings ending with soul-bleed, mind-
rage, heart-bleed-ink, paint life,
beautiful pain.

You are ascetic-joy. As life left
no joy, no walking around life outside
those skeletons.
Our lives
like discarded tattoo needles.

You were there: pain,
arms spread wide
to death,
to spirit
transforming us.

The flowers refashion old hurts,
eulogies bloom as inked narratives.
Passionate lives lived amid
pain. Deeply loved pain: joy mingled with
dust to dust fragments of spirit.

Breathe
Sandy Bezanson

I.

"LIE BACK PLEASE, the doctor is on his way and we are trying to contact your husband." The nurse flashes me a compassionate smile as she adjusts my IV drip. "And try not to worry."

Try not to worry? I might as well try not to breathe.

They can't find the heartbeat of my nearly-to-term baby on the monitor. The familiar whoosh, whoosh, whoosh under the band across my belly, the sound of the fast little heartbeat that has been my companion for days is now silent. Try not to worry.

Yet this heightened awareness of my senses cannot be compared to the fluttering feeling before I give a speech or drive through a blizzard. I can hear the whoosh, whoosh, whoosh in my mind; I know the rhythm and cadence of it as surely as I feel the beat of my own heart.

The quiet, the absence of that pattern of life-affirming sound wounds me. Is terrifying.

Breathe. Breathe. Breathe.

The doctor is not in the hospital; I know from hurried words passed between the staff in the hallway.

My husband left not an hour ago after a morning visit.

I am alone, never more so, with the quietness.

How can the lack of something be so visceral?

Okay, let's not panic then. Maybe the monitor is not operating properly or the young nurse has positioned the band incorrectly. That's right; it could be just a technical glitch. They happen all the time, don't they? It doesn't have to be bad news, the kind of extreme bad news that I won't let myself even contemplate.

Breathe breathe breathe.

Okay, look around the room; see the pink and yellow tulips that after almost a week of being in hospital, "just for a little rest, so we can keep an eye on you and monitor the baby," still look pretty. Don't dwell on the enlarged stamens, the over ripe spread of the petals, the hint of approaching decay. The flowers continue to please, yes, they have time and life left in them yet.

Breathe.

In and out, keep the rhythm, keep the rhythm…whoosh, whoosh, whoosh.
Oh, God.
God. Yes, God. Please hear my prayer. My prayer for…no, I can't ask for that, because I can't think of that, not yet.

Breathe breathe breathe.

But Mary, the Mother. Mary, you see me and hear what is in my heart. Can you find the rhythm with your Mother's soul? Mother Mary, help me now. NO, don't help me! Help my baby. The concern for myself doesn't even register compared to the vigorous and exacting fear for my child. Mary, please, the rhythm?

Breathe breath breathe.

Look at the flowers.
Breathe.

See the clock on the wall; hear the rhythmic tick tock that kept me awake on the first few nights in this room. The troubling silence has only existed for a short space of time.
The doctor will arrive and sort this out. He is caring, if not kind, and exudes reassurance, pats a hand here, bestows a crinkled wink there. The doctor will know what to do; it is all just a big mistake.

Breathe.

Another half an hour has passed and yet all is still quiet.

My husband will be here soon, surely. He'll wrap me in one of his all-encompassing hugs and it will be all right. It? I mean he or she. The baby will be fine.

We are old school and didn't want to know the sex of the baby. The appropriate name would be bestowed after birth. Weren't we good not to care which it would be?

That is the deal, isn't it? As long as it is healthy, we don't care. Well, I don't care, but don't break the bargain!

Look at the flowers.

Breathe breathe breathe.

I shift my position, lie on my side and cocoon my belly with my arms.

There is a slight tension in my tummy, and I stiffen and try to assess. Was that a ghost of a pain, a precursor of what is to happen or a hint of what is not going to come to pass? Why don't I feel, if not pain, then something, anything? Shouldn't I know, have known, that something was amiss? Aren't mothers supposed to have a sense for these things?

Guilt. Blame. Fault. All mine.

All useless.

Look at the flowers.

Breathe.

The efficient charge nurse takes a step into my room, pauses and shuts the door. When she turns to look at me there is no expression on her face.

I take this as a good sign.

She would not be so distant if there was bad news.

But I am taken aback by her subdued tone when she speaks.

"The doctor is on his way. We expect him quite soon. How are you feeling, any changes?"

I debate mentioning the phantom pain, decide to omit my fleeting discomfort and change course. "Nurse, can you repeat the test? Maybe it will work now and we'll be able to hear the…" I can't bear to say the word "heartbeat" out loud.

Breathe breathe breathe.

The nurse purses her lips. "As I said, the doctor will arrive soon. We will wait for him. Lie back and see if you can't rest a bit."

I mumble the words, "And my husband?"

"We've not been able to reach him just yet." She straightens my bedding and glides out of the room.

Breathe.

I am suddenly freezing and welcome the warmth of the blanket, thin as it is. Whether it is nerves or fear, I shake with cold. The chilliness comes as a bleak surprise after months of flushed warmth.

I gratefully accepted the increasing girth and cocktail of ripe hormones that define pregnancy. A gift of much anticipated fecundity. Was it draining from me now?

Breathe.

II.

And so.
Now we know.
The ultrasound confirmed it.

Breathe breathe breathe.

Our baby, our little he/she has not survived.

There is no reason known at present. They will examine the placenta in time. It is supposed there was an insufficiency there. It is not known why.

The doctor himself appeared to be taken aback when he gently explained the news to us.

But I could be mistaken in that for the air of unreality that descended a scant two hours ago has distanced me from things.

Why do I focus on the minute weave pattern of the faded blue blanket and yet cannot remember the medical reason why I have to endure an induced delivery of my baby?

Breathe breathe breathe.

The doctor has left us.

My husband, brave but devastated, is making calls to family. He is a strong man with deeply held feelings and will not let himself show the extent of his pain. This is his nature and comes from the need to protect those he loves, not from any lack of sensitivity.

I tend to be noisier with my emotions. It is a type of game we play, the roles well-rehearsed and comfortable to us both. But despair has not yet touched us this closely.

Will we change places in sadness?

Breathe.

Stillborn. I have always detested that term. It is stark and chilling.

Breathe breath breathe.

I am at odds with myself. When I first heard the sad facts I wanted a C-section, an immediate clean surgical removal.

Soon after I changed my mind in a jealous, instinctual husbanding of the form within me. Every second the baby is mine is precious, if not infinitely sad.

Breathe breathe breathe.

It is a moot point. I am not well; my body cannot withstand an operation.

Breathe.

Apparently I have something with the ironically cruel name of HELLP Syndrome.[1] Again the details elude me. They are trivia in a sea of grief.

---

[1] Hemolysis, Elevated Liver enzymes and Low Platelets. A pregnancy complication that affects the blood and liver. http://www.preeclampsia.org/

The specifics are the concern of my husband. He questions the doctor further. It gives him something to say, something to concentrate on, a tangible raft of words to cling to and so, it is hoped, not be swamped in the emotional swell.

Breathe.

Our parents, grandmothers-and-grandfathers-in-waiting, are now denied. I must remember that this loss is not only mine. It will be shared by a constellation of caring family and dear friends. Just now that is cold comfort. I cannot dwell on the sadness of others, but must process the reality of the moment and of what is to come.

Breathe.

III.

And so.

The hours have passed. The daunting procedure is over.

Stillborn. A tiny boy. A never-to-be-son. Perfect, but not.

I was ill, in and out of consciousness. There were drugs, movement between rooms, blood transfusions, some pain…I don't know the sequence…
The only window of clarity is when my husband and I held our son together for a few stolen moments. His tiny body was still warm. Warm from being a part of me!
The staff was kind, gave us privacy, didn't rush.
I don't know how long we had.
It wasn't experienced in minutes.
It was a piece out of time; a slice of this is all you will ever have.

It strikes me as odd that this opening of the soul is called closure. How am I to breathe when there was not breath in my child?

IV.

Looking around my room I note that the nurses were either practical or kind, perhaps both, and have removed every reminder of being in a maternity ward. Gone are the little diapers, cream and baby blankets which had been so neatly arranged in anticipation.

The tulips have also been discreetly removed.

There is only the clock to mark the long barren hours of the quiet nights.

Breathe.

It is not possible to obliterate the sound of newborn cries, or the glimpses of baby car seats filled with tiny occupants that flash past the window by the door. Sweet babies going home.

Breathe.

I haven't cried yet, not really. Well, except for the deluge that occurred upon hearing my father's voice. He said my name and I dissolved, although not in my usual loud sobs. It was more a constriction and spasm of the throat. I managed a few words, but it doesn't do to inflict your violent grief on another, not when they hurt more for your pain.

The distance of strangers is easier to bear.

Breathe.

We now inhabit a strange kind of in-between place that has an awkwardness about it. Our devastating reality has morphed into a social dilemma for others. It is the loss of what might have been, potent, for all that it could be worse. It is true, and I acknowledge it freely; to have had our son, loved, cared for and known him as a baby, or child and then to have lost him would be infinitely more crushing.

Yet it is hard to be thankful for this.

Breathe breathe breathe.

I have become irrational, like a spoiled child repeating her demand for a denied treat.

The phrase, I want my baby, plays like a demented mantra in my head.

I do not speak of this to others.

This rawness cannot last.

Breathe.

Breathe.

Breathe.

Nameless
Melanie Flores

The cramps were unmistakable
eight weeks in—not a good sign.
Behind closed doors I delivered you.
So flawlessly sculpted, lying
at the bottom of the toilet bowl.

How could there be something wrong
with such perfection?
I knew you were a girl, and I knew
that you weren't meant to be.

I swept you out of the wetness—
held your tiny, lifeless body
for the first and only time—
then buried you among the roses
where flowers grow and thorns persist.

Contract Expired
Yvonne Trainer

I.
She stands in a half empty parking lot
holding a shoe box full of pens in her left hand
a handful of books in the right.
Given to detail, she notes:
glint of sun on cars
silence of the evergreens
a shadow like a stain on the House of Learning.

The pen is mightier than the sword.

II.
Even in sleep she stands in a room full of empty desks
her handwriting fills the board in sentences
that make no sense. She turns and
a chairman whom she's never met
bursts through a back door she didn't know was there
marches to the front of the room, stares at her, and disappears.

The pen is mightier than the sword.

III.
She thinks
of school uniforms on a line
  the blazers still stained with blood.
of war nurses
  leaning over tubs of water
  to scrub away stains on young men's uniforms.
of Walt Whitman
  leaning forward to kiss the wounds of young soldiers.

The pen is mightier than the sword.

IV.
There is no end to death
In Pakistan:
 Taliban terrorists kill 145, mostly children
In Russia:
 "334 white balloons were set to the sky"
In Rio de Janeiro:
 A gunman opened fire killing twelve children, before shooting
 himself. "He left a suicide note"
In La Loche, Saskatchewan:
 Four people killed at a school. An unnamed number missing
In Connecticut:
 Twenty children killed, "He had already killed his mother, whose
 guns he stole. He killed himself at school."
These are the details. They continue.

The desks are broken
There is blood on the wood, on the windowsills, on the walls.
There are holes in the blackboard, fallen plaster on the floors.
The windows are smashed. Pages from books are scattered
like wings torn from gulls. There is one blue pen, cap missing,
left on an open book on the one upright desk.

The pen is mightier than the sword.

Quicksand
Shannon Kernaghan

Quicksand
forms in saturated loose sand.
When the sand suddenly agitates,
when water can't escape, a liquefied soil loses
strength and no longer supports weight.
When a constable knocks on our door
before we've had nearly enough sleep
you look at me with your scribble of eyebrows, dry
lips parted at these two young men in uniform, cheeks
bloodless with the heft of what they must deliver.

It takes minutes before I can process
the sounds from one man's mouth
focus on razor rash instead, his neck
blotched pink and irritated where his Adam's apple bobs,
realize your fingers are strangling my wrist
until feeling leaves my arm, next my legs.
Two found together, also a male youth, he says.
More words. Too late for Narcan, too late for interventions
her thin body unable to support the weight
of a few grains of poison.

I learn, later, that a skiff of snow blankets her arm
outstretched from the truck's open window,
nothing the rescue team can do in the inky dark parking lot
outside an Esso station after a clerk finds them,
phones it in.
         Too late.
How cold she must have been.
Was she reaching out for help?
How could I not see this? How could I not support her weight?

Heavy Metal
Shannon Kernaghan

You drop her clothes at the furthest
Salvation Army drivable in one day.
You sell her old truck in the next city.
Give it away
to the first keen Craigslist shopper who phones
or you might have left it in a ditch, keys in ignition.
You present her Kangoo Jumps and pink arm weights to friends
who accept these heavy-metal gifts with
arms reluctantly extended.

You awaken each night washed in moonlight
bathed in perspiration.
What if you spot a girl wearing her maroon sweater?
What if her half-ton drives past when you walk to the lake?
What if your friends never phone again, too burdened by your
    watery pain?
What if you see her every day?

Batgirl
Louisa Howerow

My daughter at three in her cape,
and blue t-shirt with its black appliqué,
her arms outstretched, believed
she could fly. I watched laughing,
wanted to breathe the air she breathed.
At thirteen she learned how, flew off,

while I ever fearful searched underpasses,
city alleys, kept pleading with the lost,
the dispossessed who might have heard

the scratch-flap of a bat trapped in an attic,
an abandoned warehouse. Bats, I repeated,
nurture, reach for their own at night. How do I
become a bat? One of her own? Hear
her inaudible sound—the chirps,
the sliding note? My own was constantly

stopped in my throat. I could say now
I knew why she left, remember when
she came back, say it was something I did

or didn't. I could lie. Instead for so long after
I kept tiptoeing around her, still afraid
She'd leave, still not sure what to say, do.

Today the age I was when she left, she brings
photos, a diptych—a mother, smiling, looking out
of her frame toward her Batgirl at three,

arms outstretched ready to fly. I place
the photos between us, extend my arms to hers.
It's enough, and no small thing.

Thoughts 2
Doris Charest

Daughters
Joan Shillington

I say daughter
and think water
womb-warm brooking
down my thighs
the push and whoosh
shattered mirrors
salted pain
wax and wane
moon-slave
sun-slave.
I say daughter
and knots unhook
my thoughts
dear God
daughters
rainbow prisms
Easter lilies
bloom translucent.
I say daughter
and think water
soft as slippers
on silk
oceans swoosh
swoop, swirl
surfs curl
sand, stones.

Daughters, I think
ancient light.
Grace.

To Say a Prayer
Susan Ouriou

I KNEEL DOWN beside my bed and bow my head. My hands are clasped in front of me, just like one of the pictures in my *Children's Book of Saints.* I think I'd make a good saint. "Now I lay me down to sleep, I pray the Lord my soul to keep…" After that, *we* say, "Thy love be with me through the night and wake me with the morning light." Genna Lee next door says, "If I should die before I wake, I pray the Lord my soul to take." Mom raises her eyebrows. I know, it gives me the creeps.

Maybe when I'm older I won't say my prayers out loud, kneeling by the bed. But I'll still say them. In my head. It's funny all the things that go on in there. I'm talking all the time. Not just to You but to myself or whoever I'm with, saying the things I really want to say but can't. Mom says everyone does it. Everyone walks around with a little voice in the back of their head that makes them smile or frown at the strangest times. Maybe that's what's happened to her. Maybe her little voice has just got so loud that she can't hear anyone else. I wish it would stop.

This morning when I woke up, she was screaming. I didn't know it was Mom at first. All I heard were the screams. Again and again. I ran down the hall. Her mouth was open, her arms waving in the air. Dad was beside her, trying to hold her still. She caught sight of me.

"Mommy?"

"Get away from me you, whoever you are. The pills. I've got to have the pills." She glared at Dad, "I saw you. You stole them." She screamed in his face, "Give them back."

"Nobody stole your pills," Daddy tried to make his voice soothing, like he was talking to a crying baby. "You've taken two now and everything's going to be fine. Mandy, hon, you go on to bed."

I backed away. Lori stood in the doorway to his room. He looked as scared as I felt. I kept on backing up, until I was at my door. Then I ran and dived under the covers. Mom was still screaming. Maybe to drown out the voice in her head.

I was shaking. I shouldn't have been, with all the blankets I had on top. But even their weight couldn't stop me.

Footsteps in the hall. My dad's voice. I could barely recognize it either. He was almost whimpering as he ran by. "What am I gonna do? What am I gonna do?"

I stretched the pillow tight over my head. If only I were deaf I'd hear no screams, no whimpers. I wondered about Lori. But I was too scared to go to him.

Somehow Dad got Mom to go to bed. She slept most of the day. I went in once to take her some ginger ale. She didn't know me. I didn't know her.

Please, God, let her be better tomorrow.

I sit stiff in the backseat of the car. Look straight ahead. Lori, too. Dad's dropping us off at school on his way to take Mom to the doctor's. The car inches and lurches forward. Kids stop and stare at us, at the swinging car door. I don't stare back.

"For God's sake, Shirley, leave the car door shut." Mom looks at Dad, not understanding a word. He leans over for the tenth time, yanks the door shut and locks it. You'd think the people who made cars would have thought of this. Made cars with adult-proof front doors, just like the child-proof doors in the backseat. I guess adults aren't supposed to forget what doors are for or open them in the thick of traffic, like Mom.

It takes forever but we finally make it to school. I kiss Dad goodbye. Mom is busy rolling the window up and down, her eyes and head following it all the way. Lori runs ahead of me.

We're early. I go into the compound to get away from the cold. Another girl from my class is already there. I have to tell someone. So I tell her. That my mom doesn't know who I am. That she's like a little kid. That she acts like she's never seen a car before. The other girl doesn't say anything. She looks at me strangely when I'm through. Now I really don't have anything left to say.

By the end of school, everyone points when they see me. My friends start walking home without me. I run to catch up, but they see me coming and start running themselves. I should stop right there. Pretend it doesn't matter. But it does. When they get to Dawn's house, they all run inside. It only takes me a minute to catch up. I pound on the door. No one comes to open it. I ring the doorbell. I can hear giggling inside. I keep on pounding and ringing, not knowing what else to do. Finally, I give up and start home on my own. My side aches. Lori's coming down the street. Alone. I wait for him. We walk home together. He has a black eye.

Mom is a Sunday school teacher at church. She was my teacher last year. The other kids all like her. It was neat being the teacher's kid. She's the one who started me saying my prayers every night. And now...Is it that voice inside her that drowns out all others? Or is it Your voice? Is it because I yelled at her last week? I really didn't mean it. You know that. It's just that sometimes she always seems to take Lori's side, especially when Dad's been away for this long. But there's other times she takes my side. It's no big deal. What do You want me to do?

She doesn't scream anymore. She talks. All the time. None of it makes any sense. All about people and things I have a hard time believing exist. Dad hasn't gone back to work. Even he doesn't know when she'll be better.

"What's that flickering on the screen? What does it mean? I can't see."

She scares me. I go to turn off the TV.

"No, don't do that. I've got to watch. Men, lots of men. They have guns."

"It's just a cops and robbers movie, Mom. That's all. Just cops and robbers."

"What's that noise?" Her voice is shriller now. "Bang, bang, bang. Bang, bang, bang."

I want to shut it off. Throw it out.

We eat supper—Dad, Lori and me—while Mom turns circles around us through the kitchen, living room, dining room, then back again. Around and around. I'm not hungry. Dad says I have to eat. I'm just reaching for an Oreo cookie when she stops turning. Like a toy poodle when its battery quits. With a jerk.

"Tonight I die. Bang, bang, bang." She begins to hum. The sound, like a generator, starts her on her circle path again. Round and round.

She won't die. She can't, can she? Her body's not sick. Just her mind. She can't die. Even when she doesn't know me, she's my mom. I'm only a kid. I need her. Please don't let her die. I will never, ever,

ever be bad again, I promise You. I will be the most perfect daughter on earth. But You can't let her die.

She doesn't die. This morning Mom's up before us all, opening and closing doors. I think she must have forgotten. But when I get up, she stares at me in triumph. "I didn't die," she crows, then shuts the door in my face. I feel sick. But staying home is worse than going to school. So I go. We go, Lori and me. Nobody talks to us anymore. I will never tell anyone anything again.

After school, Dad tells us we won't have to go back tomorrow. We're going to drive Mom to a special hospital a hundred kilometres away where they'll make her better. I wonder. You know on that first day? When she screamed and didn't know me? It was awful. But then, later on, when she was in bed I snuck into her room. The curtains were drawn. It was pitch black. I couldn't see anything. But she must have been able to see me.

"Mandy, come over here, honey." She knew my name! She remembered me. I ran over and threw my arms around her. "Oh, Mommy, you had me so scared and Lori too when you didn't know us, even Daddy was scared and we'd just had so much fun, with Daddy back from field camp and all of us together again, remember we went to the Y, you told me what a good swimmer I was and you just had a little headache, that's all, that's the only reason we came home early and…" Her arms around me had gone limp. I looked up, smiling, knowing I was babbling, but I just couldn't stop and then I saw her eyes and they weren't hers. I don't know whose they were. She didn't even look at me when I got up and tiptoed back out of the room.

Mom's calmer now. We don't have to worry about her opening the car door anymore. She's like a kid learning everything for the first time. Dad puts her coat on for her and buttons it up, telling her all the while about the nice car ride and how she has to keep warm. She knows we're going someplace special. She puts on lipstick. It's all crooked and smudged. Makes her face look mushed in.

She's polite with us now. She still doesn't know who we are. She knows we've been feeding her and dressing her and looking after her. We haven't hurt her. So she's polite, like with strangers. Like she never loved us or cared for us. Dad says we're the caregivers now. I want it to be the way it used to be.

Nobody says anything during the drive. We usually love car rides. Mom plays "I Spy" and "Twenty Questions" with us. Lori and I have races with the other cars. Our car always wins, mostly because in our rules any car that passes us is automatically out of the race. Dad never says much, he just drives and yells every once in a while, when me and Lori have too many fights. But today no one says a thing. I sleep a bit and wake up feeling sick. I don't tell anyone.

I don't like the hospital from the first. It has a big iron gate out front. There are green walls and black-and-white tiles on the floor. Doctors and nurses talk at us, take us from one room to another, down miles of corridors. I don't really see anyone that looks crazy. Mom doesn't even look crazy. But that's what it is, a loony bin. Or that's what the kids at school will say. I pretend I'm not really here.

It's all over so fast. Suddenly we're in front of a closed door. "This will be your wife's room," the orderly says and he takes out a big ring of keys. The door swings open onto a tiny room. It has two single beds with a nightstand between them. On the bed closest to the door sits a lady. She's the skinniest lady I've ever seen, almost like her skeleton's showing already. Her eyes don't see us.

The orderly takes Mom by the elbow and leads her over to the other bed, motions for her to sit down. She smiles and obeys. He leans over and yells at her as if she were deaf, "Shirley, your family will be back to see you in a week's time. Say goodbye now." Mom, still smiling, raises her hand and waves at us. It's only when the orderly turns his back that she starts to look confused. Just when he gets to the door, pushing us outside in front of him, she half-stands. She looks scared. Really scared. She reaches out. The door shuts. Locking her in. Locking us out.

Scared feelings. Whenever I get them, Mom tells me to say a prayer. And it works.

I bow my head. Close my eyes. But…

What if…what if I say a prayer and nothing happens? What then?

I unclasp my hands and look out the window. For the first time ever I wonder if anyone is really listening. I don't think I want to know.

To Have Children
Louisa Howerow

My daughter, knife in hand, scores
a pomegranate, top to bottom, splits it
in a bowl of water, where I'm to squeeze

each quarter, release the red translucent seeds.
She runs the blade tip lightly down her lifeline,
speaks of age, her worry—will she have children—

though she's not much older than a girl herself.
The off-white pith floats through my fingers,
seeds at the bowl's bottom I'm yet to swish clean,

to drain. I blurt, "Not me. Never wanted them."
She points the paring knife at my breast. "But you did."
I scoop out a spoonful of seeds, a glistening offer,

as if this will help explain the why of it. The fear
that having children might bring out the child
still in me, the one who used her fists. Between us

the slippery globules. Stupid maybe or maybe not,
my telling. I touch the blade, want it to puncture skin.
"The sweet mystery is I wanted you."

Marrow
Darcie Friesen Hossack

FRIEDA STEPS from the bottom stair onto the creakiest board of the old wood floor. She knows how to reach the kitchen without making a sound, but these days her mother startles easily. It's better when she knows what's coming.

The first creak is a warm-up. The next floorboard groans out Middle C, and from there she stretches to stand on each note in the broken chord.

Over the years, the notes have changed from sharp to flat as the nails loosened, though never deviated far enough to change keys.

"We should have that floor tuned," says Frieda's mother, who's struggling with the weight of a teapot. She allows Frieda to take the handle and pour.

For a time, since the last round of chemo, things seemed to be going well. Marie's platelet count had climbed, colour returned to her skin. Now, though, Marie has shrunk back down to her bones, thin as the bone china that cups her morning chamomile.

At three o'clock this afternoon, they're meant to visit Creekside and make the final payment on the Marie Reimer Package. "A light embalming," as Marie calls it. A simple birch casket, wallpapered inside using leftover rolls of tangerine damask. A ticked cushion, which Frieda sewed from an old farm quilt.

On top of the casket will be roses, not because they're anyone's favourite, but are in season.

Once Marie's been prepared, there will be a trip in the hearse, from the funeral home to Bridgeway Church, where the Mennonite Brethren have agreed to stand in the gap between the Old Colony folks who will come in from the country, and those from the Catholic church to which Marie lately converted.

"We have time for another practice run before we leave, don't you think?" Marie says.

Suddenly Frieda regrets coming downstairs.

"I thought you were happy with what we did yesterday."

"Happy, yes. But practice makes perfect. Not so much mousse

this time." Marie sits down at the kitchen table with her back to Frieda.

Almost the minute Frieda arrived home last month, her mother announced that Ms. Dyck, who had been Creekside's beautician for decades, had retired. Marie didn't trust the new hair and makeup girl to get things right.

"We'll just have to do it ourselves," Marie had said.

And then they fought.

"I don't want my hands to remember you cold. I'm sure if I talk to the girl, tell her exactly what you want, she'll do just fine. They wouldn't have hired her otherwise."

Marie has never stopped being disappointed that Frieda dropped out of the beauty college in town to go to music school out east. Halfway through learning about how to position rollers so the curls fell in the right directions, Frieda'd announced she couldn't stand the feel of other people's scalps. Either thick and spongy as fried pork rinds, or thin and tight as though already in rigor.

Frieda had won that argument by leaving home.

They both knew she wasn't going anywhere this time.

"They poached the new girl from North End," Marie had said simply.

The fight ended there.

Now, Frieda goes into the living room and opens the piano bench. Inside are her hair scissors and other tools, where she'd put them three years ago, after emptying out her music and theory books.

Back when Frieda was in grade school, she and Marie used to eat breakfast together at the kitchen table where Marie now sits. Rice Krispies popped softly in matching cereal bowls as they passed the newspaper back and forth.

"Here's one," Frieda said, snapping the freshly delivered *Prairie Post* to keep it from slumping. "Meeks, Dorothy. Born February 27, 1939, in Kyle, Saskatchewan, passed away September 22, 1984. Arrangements in care of Creekside Memorial Home."

It was the Holy Grail. A forty-five-year-old woman. For a minute, Frieda thought her mother wasn't going to make her go to school that day. But then, Marie stood and took their bowls to the kitchen, rinsed the cereal down the sink. "Best hurry," Marie said. "Can't be late for Homeroom."

When the three o'clock bell rang that afternoon, Frieda was first out the door, the zipper on her knapsack not quite closed, a crumpled bouquet of homework photocopies bunched into the front pocket.

Creekside, which was not actually beside the creek, but several blocks from it, sat directly across the street from her school, Mable Brown Junior High, where Frieda had just gone into the eighth grade. From her side of the crosswalk, Frieda could already see Marie waiting for her at the bottom of the front steps that led up to the funeral home.

Inside, a cozy gloom enveloped Frieda, blocking out the September afternoon just on the other side of the front doors. Frieda stood a moment, to let her vision adjust, even though she could have made her way through the uncomplicated warren of viewing rooms with her eyes closed.

When she could see again, she realized that Marie had gone ahead.

"Is that her?" Frieda asked when she caught up.

"Just look," Marie said, as much to herself as Frieda. "This is why it pays to go to a place that does good work."

Dorothy Meeks looked restful. Her face was relaxed, only lightly manipulated into an almost smile. Soft chestnut curls framed her face, but were cropped neatly at the nape of her neck. She wore a mauve pantsuit, the kind that could be worn either to the mall or an evening event at church without looking either too dressy or plain.

Frieda didn't need to ask whether to get out the camera. She reached into Marie's purse for their Instamatic, advanced the film, stood back, stood a little taller and snapped. The flash bulb momentarily blinded them both.

"Why don't you let me cut it for you instead of doing a perm? Something short and stylish," Frieda says, standing behind her mother and looking into their reflection in a round mirror set on the table. It's flipped to the magnifying side and the two of them are distorted as if seen through a watery window.

"We did a trim when you came home," Marie says.

Frieda knows her mother doesn't want to do something now that she'll regret. Marie intends to go into the ground with a good perm and the nut-brown rinse Frieda gets from her friends at the salon in the mall. The ones who finished school.

Frieda gathers what's left of her mother's hair into her hands. There's more of it than there was a month ago. Still, it's uneven and brittle and Frieda worries it won't survive the rollers and chemicals.

"Maybe I should just curl it with the iron when it's time," Frieda says.

"If we do that, the curls will be out before they cover me over. A perm will last forever. But I think we can wait another week," Marie says. "Remember to ask Dr. Minhas what he thinks when we see him tomorrow. He might say we have a little time yet."

Frieda plugs in her most slender curling iron, which she uses to simulate the fresh chemical curls her mother loves so much. It's pointless to suggest something more modern. Since Dorothy Meeks, Marie has known how she wants to look when she takes her place in her family album, next to her own mother and older sister, both of whom died of leukemia at the same age.

Reimer women live for forty-five years.

It used to be Frieda's job to take pictures of all the women who died at the right age. Over time, though, Marie had become more particular. They had to be just right. No big hair, false lashes or blue shadow. Blonde and red-haired women were also omitted. Those with premature wrinkles, with rosacea or a sheen of relaxed palsy, or if they were more than ordinarily well-looking or wasted away.

Some of those things couldn't be helped. But blue eye shadow alone had been enough to make them stop visiting the North End Funeral Home. At North End, everyone from ancient men who'd stroked in the night to toddlers who slipped under the creek ice in winter and were dredged up days later were given the same treatment: pinkish primer, chalky powder, whorls of rouge. Cheap hairspray that lay over their heads like halos of spider mite silk.

At Creekside, women were styled with dignity. Men never looked like women. Babies had a bit of apple brushed onto their cheeks, that's all. And if a girl was the right age and her parents requested it, they'd pierce her ears with little studs. Hearts or stars or plain gold balls.

Pierced ears was one of two birthday presents Frieda received when she turned thirteen.

"Doesn't hurt at all," said Ms. Dyck as she held a potato behind Frieda's earlobe: a pincushion to catch the sewing needle used to make the holes.

It hurt plenty.

"Well, dear," said the woman, who patted Frieda on the knee and smiled. "You're the first one who's complained."

Over the years, Frieda had learned a lot of ways a person could die. Not just middle-aged women, like Dorothy Meeks, who mixed ammonia and bleach while cleaning.

Young people, too.

A high school boy died at the annual Sidewalk Jamboree when he inhaled compressed helium directly from the canister, and his lungs burst in his chest. A girl was shipped home in a crate after her missionary parents took her to Africa and she was bitten by a cottonmouth. Twin boys killed separately, but on the same day. The first laying pennies on railroad tracks. The other quietly playing fort in his grandfather's silo when loaded grain trucks returned from the fields.

Old men died from heart attacks. Even older women just reached the end of long lives and died of death. Like Old Maid Goosen, who Frieda discovered when she left her mother alone with Dorothy Meeks.

Old Maid Goosen looked better in her casket than the last ten times Frieda had seen her at church, or even last Saturday at the Mennonite Village's Rollkuchen[1] and Watermelon Festival, where she'd been propped up in a row of other slumped, wheel-chaired ancients. Her teeth were in today, which was the biggest improvement. A woman simply can't look her best with sunken cheeks.

Frieda reached over the edge of the casket and patted the woman's hand, congratulated her on her dress, black with flowery trim at the wrists and neck. Well chosen.

---

[1] Rollkucken is flat, rectangular, deep-fried dough usually served with watermelon. Despite the name, in texture, it is more like bread than cake.

The last dress Marie will wear is pale, cornflower blue. It has been dry cleaned and hangs, still draped in plastic film, in Frieda's closet. Frieda hasn't been able to make herself hang any of her own clothes on the same rod. She keeps the closet door closed and her suitcase in front of it. Her shirts, jeans, skirts and a single dress hang in front of the window, instead, darkening the room. If she could, she would cover the walls and every last inch of wallpaper with her clothes.

Frieda pushes aside her suitcase, takes her mother's dress out of the closet and holds it against the tangerine damask walls.

Frieda chose the pattern for her room when she was thirteen. She hadn't known her mother kept two extra rolls for herself.

There were three viewing rooms at Creekside.

After visiting Dorothy Meeks and Old Maid Goosen, Frieda went into the third room. In an impossibly small casket, a baby girl was laid out. Skim milk skin revealed a web of blue veins. Rosebud lips. Lashes curled onto plump cheeks, like butterfly legs. She'd been dressed in white eyelet cotton and hand-knit booties tied with perfect satin bows. Much better than the little sailor suits or satin gowns mothers often chose for big occasions.

There was no mother in sight today, though, besides Frieda's. So when air conditioning began to pour in from a vent overhead, making Frieda shiver, she looked over her shoulder to make sure no one was watching, and tucked the baby girl under a chenille blanket that had been left folded over the side of her casket.

Although she knew her mother would tell her to stop wasting film, Frieda snapped a picture of the baby girl, then went back to take one of Old Maid Goosen.

Afterwards, Frieda and Marie went to Piccadilly's on Central Avenue and Frieda ordered her usual: a scoop of Black Forest and one of Double Fudge. In a cup not a cone, with a cherry on top. For supper Marie roasted marrow bones, the familiar smell of scorched minerals giving way to a meaty aroma as the pink pulp of fat and blood turned to tunnels of beige, animal jelly.

If the bones cooked too long, the marrow would liquefy, leaving the bones empty, with nothing to scoop out onto toast.

The trick was to know when it was time.

Four days later, when Hegg's Drugstore called to say the pictures were ready, Frieda slipped the baby and Old Maid Goosen from the envelope and brought her mother the rest. Usually Marie taped the women into a scrapbook, but Dorothy Meeks was different. Instead of becoming part of a catalogue, Marie daubed the back of the photograph with a bit of Frieda's school glue stick and lightly fastened it inside the family photo album, next to Frieda's grandmother and aunt.

Fourteen years later, Dorothy Meeks is still filling in. Frieda wonders what the woman's family would think.

Later that night, Marie lies in bed. Her fingers alternately reach up to touch her perfectly curled hair and move over the string of rosary beads she carries with her everywhere.

She'd grown up Mennonite, of course. Spent most of her life wishing for a few beads of comfort, and on Sundays, a church with some stained glass to dress up an otherwise plain wood box.

The day Marie had her first nosebleed, two years ago now, she had walked to the clinic and waited her turn. Listened to the on-call doctor tell her to be optimistic. As she walked home, she turned down a different street than she usually took. Without meaning to, she followed a group of women up the stairs to Christ the Redeemer Church on Circle Avenue and sat through her first Mass. She found rosary beads abandoned on the pew and took them home with her. Six months later she converted, so she could both confess to their theft and carry them without feeling like a fraud.

The last thing Marie remembers of her own mother, already forty years old when Marie was born, is being lifted up by a family member to see inside her casket. A moment later Marie was set back down and didn't move from that spot. She stood facing the planed and plumb wooden sides of the box, as those gathered recited hymns in German. She stood while an uncle with an AutoMagic camera snapped a picture to go next to Marie's mother's wedding photograph. In both, her hair is scraped over her head into a bun, and around her waist is tied the same white apron over the same black dress.

Marie didn't leave her mother's side, even when everyone went to the front of the house for buns and cold pork. Even after the horse-drawn hearse arrived in front of their door and took her mother, Marie stood, until she fell asleep on her feet and someone carried her away, too.

Over the next years, Marie often returned to the place where she'd stood.

"Something should be done about that one," her father remarked to Marie's older sister, until she gave Marie the photo album that contained their mother's last picture. After that, Marie never went into the room again.

Not until she stood over her sister who, in death, wore the same grey bun as their mother.

When Marie and Frieda return home from their appointment at Creekside, Frieda helps her mother upstairs and into bed, covers her body with a quilt that suddenly feels too heavy. She closes the door softly as she retreats into the hallway.

A few steps away is the bathroom. Frieda goes in and locks the door before turning on the tub and sink faucets as hot as they will go. She sits on the toilet lid, hugs her knees to her chest and rests her head. She always forgets how dry it is in Saskatchewan, having grown accustomed to Ontario's brothy air. Every day since coming home, Frieda has had to hide at least one nosebleed from her mother. Marie would never believe a bit of dry wind could be all that was the matter.

Spring
Liz Kingsley

There was the spring
they woke up tall with biceps.
The spring when their voices
plunged. The spring we felt
stubble on their cheeks. The
spring when they hugged us hard
like men. The spring when they moved
heavy boxes from the attic. The spring
we made them steak and chicken and
they were still hungry. The spring when
they first thrust their tongues into strange
girls' mouths. The spring when they took
AP History and taught us what caused the wars.
The spring when they passed the driver's test
and backed into parked cars. The same spring
they bought themselves condoms, large.
The spring when they tucked us into bed
and stayed up into the wee hours. The spring
when they learned to shake hands and
wore khakis. The spring when we let them
drink with us. The spring when they asked
how our day was. It was the spring they opened
chequing accounts. The spring they had a boss.
The spring the future was on their minds. The
spring we prayed their mistakes wouldn't cost
them too much. It was the spring of thawing
and blooming we thought would never get here,
the spring we prayed that winter would return.

Bigfoot Therapy
Barb Howard

S URE, THERE WAS an element of surprise when Bigfoot gently
plucked Josie off her bike and enveloped her in his arms. But she
didn't feel fear. She felt a hug, really. A hug with just enough squeeze,
just enough warmth. The hair on Bigfoot's arms and torso was as soft
as an angora comforter. And right away Josie liked the smell of him.
He smelled a bit like popcorn—the way a dog's paws often do.

Bigfoot held her for a moment, then he set her on the ground. Josie
stood there, a little wobbly, missing the hug, while Bigfoot retrieved
her bike, which had rolled down the trail a short distance, and carried
it back to her. After giving her the bike he held out his huge paw-
hands as if to say "sorry, sorry, I don't know what came over me." Then
he backed off the trail into the bush. He gave Josie a short wave,
turned and walked deeper into the forest.

Josie looked at the trail ahead of her, the same trail she rode every day
after dinner, the haze of dusk beginning to settle on it. She thought
of her house, full of good memories but empty of people, waiting for
her at the end of the ride. Then she thought of Bigfoot's hug. She
pushed her bike off the trail and into the trough of flattened bushes.
Bigfoot was easy to track.

Before the Bigfoot hug, Josie had been biking a section of narrow
single track, a few tight-banked corners, the trail dotted with
yellowing poplar leaves. And she'd been riding hard, ignoring that
slow leak in her front tire, trying to keep up enough speed so she
didn't know if her eyes watered from wind or weeping. Or if her
nose ran from adrenaline or crying. Pedaling was a release from the
hollowness that had been inside her for months—since her kids left,
the two of them, best buds, leaving together in a blur of duffle bags,
idealism and brotherly trash talking, for college in the north. The
older one had stayed home to work and wait for the younger one to
finish school. And now they were off. Josie knew that this was good.
Her kids had grown up, reached adulthood. She knew that they were

a lucky family living the dream, that things could not have turned out any better. But still. She missed them in such an embarrassing pathetic fashion that she could not voice it aloud. She was ashamed to be that woman who, after they left, plugged in their weird dubstep music and sat at the kitchen table and cried as she rolled up the extra placemats—and yes, that woman who any onlooker would look upon and say, oh for God's sake, first-world problem, suck it up.

And then, as if the kids leaving wasn't enough, there was the dog. Josie had counted on the dog as a companion for at least another year. He was old and his neck and the area behind his ears had begun to smell like canned tuna. After waking up from a nap he would seem shocked that he'd left a tiny pee puddle on the floor. His death wasn't a grim tragedy, just another natural trajectory. But still. The dog's death, like the kids leaving, surprised Josie. Even though it shouldn't have. The dog had wrapped himself around the wheeled legs of her chair every morning while she worked—which may have shown, as the kids said, that the dog did not have a vestige of animal survival instincts—but it made Josie feel grounded to have him there weighing down her chair. Somehow it even made Josie feel like her work mattered—like she should keep at it, because if she stopped suddenly and stood up she might roll over and crush the dog's tail or thin legs.

And then there was Josie's husband. Well. No hanging out with a weepy wife for him. He had animal survival instincts. He moved right in with his own Bigfoot. Young Stiletto-Foot from the office. Such a cliché that Josie should have seen it coming. Good riddance. Still. Her husband was good at making omelettes and doing laundry. His footsteps and sports radio and overlong showers had taken away some of the unwanted, unbroken hush in the house.

Josie caught up with Bigfoot at a backwoods pond—an oasis of thick moss and purple fleabane. Bigfoot was at the edge of the pond pulling bulrushes. Josie sat on the ground near him and wrapped her arms around her knees. She watched Bigfoot working, and she listened as the crickets began their evening chorus, and she tried to think of a reason why she should go home. As night fell she stretched out on the ground, used her knapsack as a pillow. Bigfoot left the pond, a stack of bulrushes under one arm. When he walked by Josie he stooped to cover her with a moss blanket. Before she closed her eyes, Josie watched Bigfoot crawl under a fir tree, eat the bulrushes, and then curl up to sleep.

The next morning, Bigfoot used his paw-hands to indicate that Josie could travel with him if she wanted. Josie nodded, and they were on the move together. Bigfoot never threatened or restrained Josie. She could leave anytime. He carried her bike over his shoulder, but he wasn't keeping it from her. He carefully buckled her helmet onto the crossbar, and when they rested or camped at night he leaned the bike against a tree or laid it on the ground, gear side up, always protecting the derailleur, almost as though he knew it was a fragile part. Josie was thankful that Bigfoot carried her bike. The terrain they travelled, through the thickest brush and hidden creek-sides of the foothills, was mostly unrideable. And there was that slow leak in her front tire. Josie knew the more she rode the bike the more likely the tire would go fully flat. She should have fixed the problem ages ago by changing the tube but, instead, she had dealt with it by topping up the air before every ride. She carried a backpack of supplies, but during the summer she had used up all her spare tubes and inflation cartridges and not bought more. Small tasks, like buying tubes and cartridges, had started to become insurmountable.

Josie knew the region that she and Bigfoot travelled. She had biked the area for decades, although until now she had no idea of the extent of the lush world beyond the trails. Sometimes Bigfoot led Josie to the edge of the trails, where they laid on their bellies and peered through the red alder and tall grass at the bikers. Many of those bikers were people that Josie recognized. Neighbours, cycling colleagues, the local plumber, the woman with braids who taught her kids biology in high school. People she might have waved to, or talked about the weather with, if she was riding on the trail, but no friends. She had a few true friends, she'd thought about calling them about this ache caused by the exodus of her household, but how would she start? How could she not be embarrassed by problems that would seem so everyday, so not problems, to the rest of the world? So, instead of talking, she biked. A lot.

Josie offered Bigfoot the dried apricots that she carried in her backpack. He declined, gestured that she should eat them all herself. After the apricots were gone, Josie ate bulrushes with Bigfoot. In her youth, once, at summer camp, Josie ate bulrushes after they'd been roasted over a fire. With Bigfoot she ate them raw. Day after day. The bulrushes, even the ones that had started to go to seed, were not that different from camp food. Not that different from the bagged salads and toast she'd been eating every night at home.

Bigfoot ate slowly, usually in silence. He didn't respond to questions, but he could mimic. He made crow calls and the squeal of bicycle disc brakes and the sound of water rushing over rocks. He made Josie laugh by puffing out his huge auburn chest and muttering small words he overheard from bikers on the trail. Nice. Dude. Wow.

Bigfoot said wow a lot.

At night, after the first night, Bigfoot and Josie spooned. Bigfoot draped his arm over Josie's body, crushing her a little, but in a cozy, companionable way. The weight of his arm squeezed out the empty space that had been overwhelming her. At home, sometimes she woke and realized she had been crying in her sleep, her eyes feeling wet and raw and unrested. It happened the first few nights with Bigfoot—and in the morning, when she wiped the dried salt tracks from her face, Bigfoot would put his paw-hand on her shoulder and nod in a way that seemed to say yes, that's okay, let it out.

After those first few nights she slept soundly beside Bigfoot. Deep restorative sleeps without tears.

One morning, Bigfoot got up earlier than usual from the low grassy nest where they slept. Josie watched him walk towards the creek, his arms swinging low and easily, his head nodding slightly side to side, as though he was listening to, or full of, music. He stopped, tilted his head and looked skyward, at a formation of geese flying across the indigo dawn. Josie watched his shoulders rise and fall with each breath. She heard him say wow. After a few moments, he dropped his gaze and continued ambling to the creek.

Josie sat up. She noticed the frost on the surrounding rye grass and fescue. Not the light frost that had appeared a few mornings ago. But a thick, hard frost that wouldn't burn off until midday. Josie wore all the spare clothes she carried in her knapsack. Her fleece, her bike tights and toque. She wasn't cold, Bigfoot's warmth lingered in the nest, but she felt the seasonal change in the air.

Bigfoot returned with Josie's water bottle, filled with creek water. He handed it to her and, sitting on his haunches, watched patiently while she drank. Then Bigfoot got her bike. Rather than carry it on his shoulder, he rolled it towards her. He patted the seat. She knew he was telling her that it was time for her to go home.

Josie gave the front tire a light squeeze. The slow leak had not yet completely deflated the tube. Somehow it had held on. There was enough air to start riding. Bigfoot undid the helmet from the crossbar and handed it to Josie. She snugged the helmet onto her head, buckled the chin strap. Then Bigfoot pointed to the trail on the other side of the bushes.

Josie pushed her bike out of the brush and onto the familiar stretch of single track. Bigfoot walked beside her. She straddled the bike and tried to smile at him. Bigfoot placed his hand on her lower back. Then, ever so softly, he gave her a tiny push. The bike began to roll and Josie began to pedal and work the shifters, the derailleur smoothly guiding the chain to the next gear.

At the first hill Josie rose out of the seat, put all her weight onto the pedals, forced the bike to keep rolling upward. She thought of her kids, her dog, her husband. In that order. Near the top of the hill she thought of herself. Yes, she was going to be all right. And as she crested the hill and saw the full expanse of sky meeting the foothills, and took in the deepening golds and reds of autumn, she felt a hint of joy rising in her heart. And she thought of Bigfoot. Wow.

What Feeds Us

Louisa Howerow

When my son moves out, he invites me
to his table, jokes that if I were left alone,
I'd be reduced to dry bread and weak tea,

a syndrome of the elderly. "I'll dip bread
in spiked tea," I tell him and take the wine
he offers, swirl it in the glass, offer a toast.
He watches for signs I'm losing weight,
losing words, sleep. This might be true.
What I don't eat he'll pack into doggy bags
and I'll remind him my kitchen holds food
for the nosher, the frugal, the widowed.
Enough for a non-cook, not for a son who

learned to talk bouillabaisse with his father,
bap and kimchi with his first girlfriend.
What I keep to myself is how yesterday
I bit into sweet dough enfolding empress
plums, their warm juices spurting, staining
my blouse, and his father was with me.

Sudden Leap Away
Joan Crate

As we drove up to the house,
it was the way the buck
peered at us that struck me
—its sombre regard—
as if that boy's spirit infused
the deer, his grace in its sudden leap

away. How did he know
what trail to take: which led
to the cliff, which to the creek
bed, the hollow of snow
to lie down and sleep in?

The antlered eyes
left wounds on our skin.
Now, I wait for him
to return, an apple in my hand.

Everything, everyone is hungry.

That bruise-coloured
whisper persuading snow
to melt into night—like him
at ten, afraid of being teased
he'd hold daylight in his lungs
until it hardened to a warning
of poor visibility and careless driving.

By sixteen he'd learned
to look past everyone
with road-weary eyes
cool as a snooze
at the wheel.

I think that really is him
in the deer, in the shade.

Saplings too. They sprung up
at the side of the road confident
at first, growing a foot a year,
conferring with peers.

One was perfectly symmetrical,
and I imagined it in years to come
strung with Christmas lights and songbirds,

a grinning green emblem of the future

until the drought came.

Needles yellowed and branches
turned brittle. The tree never recovered,
so two weeks ago we chopped it down
and stuck it in a bucket of stones—our beautiful
butchered sacrifice, a casualty of weather,
martyr to changing fortunes.

This is his winter, of course.
We can't wish *Merry Christmas*
without hearing the season of his laugh.
White roses bloom from his mouth
and form a wreath at our throats.

We choke.

All through the holidays,
he is with us in the house:
a decorated soldier, a wandering carol,
the cause and antidote of our heartbreak,
the memory of a man gone home,
his gift dropped in an empty room.

Even sundogs howl his name.

> Come Spring, flocks of birds will build
> in the branches of his absence, furnish
> their nests with the soft down
> of his footsteps walking silently
> through the corridors of our loss.

The second night of the New Year
the moon is an overblown balloon.
The stars cry bright.

Bedtime Walls Peacocks Men's-Room Stalls
Michael

I.

I am a gay man living with HIV
I have never been an alcoholic or drug user
but I have struggled
with what some would call
"sex addiction"
that said it is difficult to define,
especially within gay culture
which by its very definition
breaks down the confines
of convention
of sexual propriety

my mother struggled with
PTSD
survivor guilt
depression
after a bad car accident in her late teens.
It's only now in my thirties
in the process of making art
cathartic and painful
that I've discovered
transgenerational trauma
and its effects

exploring the residual trauma
being gay
and carrying that as a burden
(sometimes)

It's clear to me
the two feed each other
construct and deconstruct
me in an unhealthy way

despite my efforts
I was never able to make my mother
NOT want to kill herself

despite my efforts
this has translated into
feelings of inferiority
within my vessel

as a sexual being
I am a divided man

II.

The first divide I can recall
was hearing sobs through the bedroom wall
Filled with pain was my mother's plea
nightly
'Lord, why oh why won't you just take me?'

I feel his hand upon my skin
a gentle tug, a moan and more
'Take me daddy
I'm a fucking whore!'

I turned in bed to drown the sound
hid my ears
choked on tears
yelled and yelled
and yelled and yelled

Now on my knees
just waiting here
An only child
a fucking queer

Of course at times I couldn't resist
I crawled to her
and with a kiss
broke the wall
and brushed her cheek
'I'm here mommy
It's not so bleak'

His mouth's around me
throbbing hard
I've found relief
but I know I'm scarred

She'd hold me close
a midnight pause
'It's not you
my precious dear
the demons come
then they disappear'

From mouth to mouth
below the stalls
the breath of life
the parasols

So who's the mother her or me?
It's an illusion
a wayward cry
Trying so hard
to be a good boy
to quench her pain
to elicit joy

138

He fills the holes
the wholes
Left alone
they rot

III.

And then she died,
s o   u n r e s o l v e d
Her baggage bequeathed
but not absolved

Hands and places
we have no faces
men's-room stalls
standing in
for bedroom walls

Left in a lurch
I wandered round
seeking a mother
who couldn't be found
A part of me got lost so young
All alone
the only one

The walls are different
The guilt's the same
Searching for someone
to take the pain

Mothering in Lieu
Chynna Laird

A s AN ADULT looking back over my life, I know how extremely fortunate I am to be where I am today. I suppose many people thought I'd end up in the void of children from questionable childhoods pushed aside and forgotten: children who simply slipped between the cracks of a tunnel-visioned system.

I'm sure you knew one of those kids who grew up on the wrong side of the tracks surrounded by chaos of one sort or another. That kid who obviously struggled with…something. That kid no one was courageous enough to stand up for or talk to. That kid—who secretly waited for *anyone* to guide her out of her situation, someone brave enough to be positive, a person willing to help pull her out from the undercurrents tugging her back in the other direction—was me.

I was "that kid."

My mother was a young single parent raising two children. She'd chosen not to include our father in our lives, not because he was a bad guy, but more out of pride. Mom wanted to do it all on her own. Unfortunately, she wasn't strong enough to meet the job requirements most of the time.

As I grew up and finally found my voice, I told people that my mom was pulled in three different, but equally powerful, directions: her struggles with bipolar that she refused to either acknowledge or treat, the crutches she turned to that she also refused to acknowledge or treat, and her music. I still find it dumbfounding that my mother was truly one of the most talented people I've ever known, and yet she didn't allow her talent to pull her away from the other forces. Her inner battles made my life with her frustrating, confusing and, sometimes, very frightening.

But unlike other kids in similar situations, I was blessed because I didn't just have *one* person to reach out to and who reached out to me. I had *four*. Four beautiful, powerfully strong women, who each gave me a piece of mothering I needed so desperately.

My grandmother was an accomplished artist and did everything a woman wasn't supposed to do seventy years ago. She travelled, went to school, lived on her own, had a career and, shockingly, had relationships before marriage. She battled breast cancer, *twice*, and survived the disease during a time when the odds were against her. In the later stages of her life, she fought an unforgiving illness that stole us from her memory. And she did everything with grace, strength and dignity.

Grandma gave me the gifts of courage, wisdom and passion while teaching me that women had the ability to do anything, be anyone and go further than people of her era believed they should have been allowed to. And I hold her final words to me, when she still recognized my face, close to my heart: "You be true to yourself, Dumpling. I believe in you and always will."

I also had an aunt who shot from the hip and never accepted "I can't!" from me. She taught me that a woman can be strong *and* feminine *and* self-supporting, even while in a marriage. She taught me to follow my heart and to do what I love, not what others told me was safest or best for me.

Aunt Dorothy gave me the gifts of self-reliance, resilience and self-esteem. And even in times when I believed my dream was too far away, she showed me how to get there.

My loving godmother, whose pure, unconditional love and kindness restored my faith and repaired my soul, convinced me that my existence mattered. She taught me to trust the words "I love you," and that love didn't have to hurt. She believed in me during a time when I'd lost myself and had wanted to give up. She taught me to see the good, always, even when things seemed foggy.

My godmother, Auntie Lois, gave me the gifts of faith and love, not just for others but, most importantly, for myself. Because to love others, we need to love ourselves and our Higher Power (whatever that may be) *first*.

Finally, I had a beautiful stepmother, who I have never called "step." She loved me as her own from day one. She taught me about new levels of friendship, trust and family I'd never known about before her presence in my life. She showed me how a woman can balance family, work and self while being true to each. Through her I also learned that a stepmother wasn't a replacement mom but a "Bonus Mom."

Robin gave me the gifts of acceptance, self-respect and the importance of staying true to my values.

So, even though my birth mother wasn't able to mother me the way she'd wanted to, everything turned out okay. My bitterness faded long ago because I realized things could have gone a very different route.

Yes. I was "that kid." But how amazing is it that I had four fantastic women to mother me, each in her own way. Their combined gifts were the exact doses of nurturing I needed to survive, thrive and grow. I credit each of them for helping me to become the mother I am to my own four children.

These amazing women are still in my life. I don't tell them as often as I should how truly grateful I am that they never treated me as "that kid."

They were the brave ones, my mothers in lieu.

Four Generations of Stepmothers
Penney Kome

GERDA

The widest band on my ring finger, left hand, is my grandmother's ring,
left behind in her mending, under loose spools, a flash of jewels,
  a bonus pleasure. On my hand, the ring's three big old diamonds
  gleam and shine,
stones flat-cut at the mine, nineteenth-century bling—
the thick gold line between my sparkling anniversary rings, whose
  glittering diamonds measure thirty-four years of married blessings.
How I treasure Gerda's ring, from my step-grandmother,
my mother's stepmother, who became our Southern saving grace.
  Brilliant, rich, tall and to some, an old maid Gerda fell for a
  divorced man in disgrace, who asked her office for social aid.

Without Grandma Millie, Granddad was an Air Force chaplain on
  the family plan,
with three teenaged boys to take in hand. Instant family!
Gerda raised those three handily, while she finished her PhD.
Then she reached out to my mother, Granddad's defiant daughter,
  and she rescued us three, my mother, my brother, and me.

BRENDA

Brenda's last daily task before dinner was to bake fresh bread.
She started every morning by scalding the milk, feeding the yeast
making the mixer go whipping through inflatable dough,
then she set the dough in the oven to rise under a red checked disguise.
Four hearty breakfasts later, four children thundered out the door,
  headed for school, ready to learn more.
SuperMom became a super-cleaning blur, vacuuming floors, wiping
  down doors,
popping clothes and dishes into the right washers, writing cheques,
  phoning offices,
slotting doctors' appointments into calendar spots.

After sweeping, dusting, and laundry, she would open the warming
  oven, to show bowls overflowing with bread dough, puffing out
  the red-checked tops, ready to go.
Thumped out onto the floured counter, punched down and chopped
  in four if that was enough, or more if she wanted buns, the dough
  went into pans and under covers again to grow. And puff up.

As supper smells suffused the air, the dogs stirred, well aware that
  soon four kids
would sweep in like a hungry typhoon, and Dad would open the door
  and take off his hat.
Brenda was also counting down to that.
We'd hear hot oven racks ring as she slid the loaf pans in.
Then she'd pull up a chair, pour herself another glass of wine, and
  actually sit down for the first time, with fifteen minutes to go until
  the family arrived.

She'd turn on the oven light, sip her wine, and cheer as she watched
  the baking bread rise.

Brenda's cooking skills are with me still. Her search for bliss in
  domesticity eludes me though, as it did her, which perhaps played
  a part in her early death.

KIMMY
Admiring the whimsical winking cartoon owl, Kimmy fingered the
  glued repair
on the rough ceramic bowl and sighed.
"I could make you another bowl, Mom," she said, "now that my kiln
  is working again."
"I'd love a bowl from you," I said, "I'll put it next to this one."
The owl, I explained, was one of Brenda's decorating refrains, perched
  all about, on plates, cups, plaques, and flags, indoors and out.
Next to her blue-and-white tea tin, the owl plate takes up most of the
  space in my living room display I call Stepmother's Place.

Kim caught my drift with a nod, and we both found it odd, to be
   talking both as stepdaughters and as
stepmothers, nearly sisters, mothers dealing with memories of our
   own mothers and others.
Kim didn't say as she went away that she'd added the sprawly scrawly
   owl to her own artistic displays.

Kim usually likes to make images of crows, her late mother's friends,
   and the messages she sends
through her crow couriers, easily posed for portrait or sculpture.
   Kim's shelves have crows in blue boots
cawing the news, crows in trees waving their wings in the breeze, and
   painted trays with rows and rows
of strutting crows out for a stroll.

Months after her visit from the east coast, a birthday box arrived.
When I unrolled the wool, wrapped like a scroll around my palm-
   sized gift,
out fell a familiar owl's face on an oval plate, a clay pendant
on a sleek leather lace to complement my Stepmother's Place.

In my mind, I saw Kim's clever artistic hands trace the owl's outline
   once again,
grasping the design with her strong hands and incising the totem on
   hard clay.
Her artist's hands that mould lifelike masks and that mix pot glazes
   that shimmer like water.
Her tender hands that opened wide to her fiancée's daughter, and
   soothed her fears.
Her calm hands that wiped her dying mother's brow through her tears.
Kim was decades younger than I when she had to help her mother die,
Caring for her at home, for several months in a row. Kimmy kept on
   smiling through.
She wears her grandmother's diamond ring on her left hand, ring
   finger, as I do, too.

The Wing-Breath of Wasps
Joan Shillington

Two grandmas, we bundle
the boys in their red wagon
and walk the distance
for hot chocolate, huddle
beneath table umbrellas
in a rain deluge.

We watch four wasps crawl
between puddles. Grounded
drenched but still trying.
Afterwards, we visit
exotic birds and reptiles
at a pet store. Four kittens
for sale. We name them:
Rover. Ginger. Spotty. Paws.

There was a silence
within the downpour
even along Yonge Street
with Saturday traffic
and the Avenue where wet
leaves clung to the boys
as we hurried home
for supper.

And that is how the day
is taken by each little thing,
the come and go of it all,
confused by a beauty
that disguises itself
as our lives.

The Scent of Nettles
Daniela Elza

                         the scent of nettles
hurls my memory   to shady spots
to my grandmother's hands   snapping
tender tips

while the day lilies burn their life into mine

she comes back to me   every year
in her wedding habit   uncertain
of who   she truly married

unsure   if she ever walked barefoot
                              on maritime rocks

my mother   cooks nettles
she knows how to grow   a flower
in a bowl

I never knew   how much she worried

in my hands   the lilies fade
                    the fragile life   we are

my son plays   oblivious
            to the evolutionary possibilities
within this morning
            within a mirror
                        within a wheel

to him it's a glass case   I can't open
until I learn   it is okay
                        for the milk   to spill

or for me to cry when he wanders off
into nettles
                    and brings me   a daylily

holding my heart   in his hands

Nourishing Your Roots

Michelle Austen

In the Child Footsteps of Light
Daniela Elza

through regular windows   on regular days
this century-old house   still stands
                perfecting   the art of light.

still invites the day   into itself
              as if   it were sustenance.

beveled glass   turns playground
              for even a little bit of sun.
draws music out of   the language of
                    shadows.

in this house   rainbows are born.

he captures them in an old straw basket
plucks blooms   off white walls
paints them   onto pieces of paper.

child eyes record.   refine.   distill.
a rare brew   I drink from.

the light disguised in the blue furniture
is still   a mystery to   him.

he will later learn   light gives colour
and light takes   colour away.

that rainbows are   light's willingness
               to be known.

that each day   there comes a slant—
the moment when light   reveals
            the flaws   in a house.

those   even the builders   gave up on.

intimacy   begins   with this revelation.
with the smell of   burnt milk   over
                              spilled rainbows.

Halifax Public Gardens
Yvonne Trainer

A man and a woman walk at noon in the Public Gardens.
She pushes the baby in a stroller; he pushes his father in
a wheelchair.

The father is bald and skeletal. He has no teeth; his legs
have been
amputated at the knees. The baby is bald and has no teeth;
she has not

yet learned to walk. The couple park the wheelchair and
stroller side by side
facing the empty outdoor stage. They turn to buy ice cream
from a vendor.

The grandfather reaches out one bony finger. The baby
grasps it.
They grin toothless grins. A brass army band appears

ascends the stage. Gold instruments flash in the sun. The band
plays. Everyone stops.

Old-fashioned men in suits arise from the benches, take off
their hats and

hold them to their hearts. Little flocks of blackbirds fly up.
Dew dries on the grass.

The couple stand at attention, holding an ice cream cone in
each hand.
In the background

a thirsty ocean laps and laps up the music. An excited dog
wags and wags its tail.

The baby in yellow sundress tugs the old man's finger. They grin and lean forward together.

Talbot Crescent
Jane Cawthorne

At the sound of the scream, Mary scanned the yard. Out the kitchen window, she counted eight children (not all hers, thank God) huddled in the middle of a decrepit rectangle of crusty snow that was supposed to be a backyard hockey rink. Dan had meant well, but with the Auto Pact signed and all the plants in Windsor ramping up production, he never had time to flood the ice anymore. Kids being kids, they had found all kinds of ways to use the space. Today, it provided borders for a game that involved two tricycles and some lawn chairs from the shed. Then she saw it. The lawn dart game.

The huddle shifted as faces looked towards her in the kitchen window. Patty was on the ground with a lawn dart in her upper arm and that Forrester kid was about to pull it out. Mary ran into the yard in her slippers, skidded on one of the few remaining patches of ice and fell hard beside her daughter. "Don't touch it."

The Forrester kid dropped his hand from the dart. At least he had the decency to look guilty.

She should have been keeping a better eye on them.

If she picked Patty up, she might do more damage. Caroline's boy, Brian, looked like he might throw up. Mary couldn't cope with that too. "Brian, go get your mother." But Caroline was already running into the yard, snow boots pulled over black slacks and her husband's camel-coloured overcoat flapping over a chic matching turtleneck. She always looked great. Like a beatnik.

"Don't move the dart." Caroline had been training to become a nurse when she got married. "Do you want me to get Dan?" she asked.

"He's at work." There is no such thing as a weekend for a shift worker.

"Let's see what we've got here," said Mary, gently unbuttoning Patty's coat.

Caroline took charge of the other children. "Brian, take Sean and Dustin to our house. Tell your dad that if I'm not back by noon, he'll have to make lunch. There's macaroni and cheese in the cupboard. The rest of you kids, go home."

154

The little crowd dispersed. The Forrester kid mumbled, "Sorry."

"It's okay," said Mary. "I'm sure it was an accident."

The Forrester kid did not leave.

"How are we going to get her into the car without moving the dart?" Caroline asked.

"I can't see what's happening with this coat on her."

"Do you want me to get some scissors so we can cut it off?"

That would mean buying a new coat. Mary hesitated. Her teeth started to chatter. "Wait. Let me think." As she said it, the dart fell out and rolled onto the snow leaving a thin trail of blood. "Oh dear."

The Forrester kid paled.

Patty wailed again. Mary pulled Patty's arm out of the coat. Blood had seeped through her sweater.

"Okay. Let's go. She might need stitches." Caroline whipped the silky scarf from around her neck. "Tie this around her arm. I'll pull the Falcon into your driveway. Can you carry her while you get your coat?" Mary nodded and scooped Patty into her arms. The Forrester kid shadowed her to her back door and then appeared again around the front and held the door while Mary left still carrying Patty and now clutching her own coat and purse too. "It's going to be all right," she said to no one and everyone.

The Forrester kid loped towards his house in his too-big hand-me-down snow boots, shoulders rounded, head down. Other mothers, even Mavis Roth, were at their doors, watching.

Caroline and Bud, the Bremners, were the only family on the street with a second car. As a manager, Bud got a new company car every two years and last year, when it came time for a new car, he bought the '62 Falcon Squire he had been driving and told Caroline to get her licence. Caroline's good fortune caused a ripple of resentment on Talbot Crescent, especially from Mavis Roth, who had always made snide comments about Caroline's clothes, her good figure, her beautiful house, her new appliances and even her willingness to help others. At the Bremners' Christmas Open House, Mavis had looked around at the dining room table laden with treats, the sparkling decorations, the fully stocked bar and at Caroline herself and said "Well, with only one child, she has the time."

There wasn't a person on Talbot Crescent Caroline hadn't helped with that car.

155

"Look at Mavis, waving like she's my best friend."

"Oh, she's not that bad," said Caroline. Caroline never said a bad word about anyone.

If it weren't for Caroline, Mary thought she would go crazy. She couldn't even really say why. She could go next door any morning after the boys went to school and find Caroline at her kitchen table, smoking a cigarette and drinking coffee with the *Windsor Star* spread out before her. She talked to Mary as though Mary had already read the news and asked her what she thought about all kinds of things—civil rights, Malcolm X, Vietnam. Caroline would never let her get away with saying she didn't know. But sometimes she really didn't. One day Mary said, "It's not even our war."

"No, maybe not," said Caroline. "But we're in it. We're selling weapons."

Mary hadn't known that. But what did it matter? The kids were enough of a worry. Dan was too rough on Sean. A sensitive type, Dan called him. That's what had prompted the hockey rink. "Get the kid outside," Dan had said.

"What's wrong with being sensitive?" Caroline had asked. "Would you rather he was insensitive?" Caroline always had a different perspective and once Mary heard it, she wondered why she had never thought of it herself. Last week, Dustin tried to take apart the television. He had a screwdriver in his hand and was tinkering away at the back of it when she found him. All Mary could think about was that he could have been electrocuted. Maybe she didn't pay enough attention to him. That could happen with the middle child. When she asked him what he thought he was doing, he said he wanted to let the people out. When she told Caroline, Caroline laughed so hard about it, she made Mary laugh too. She called him "Dustin the Liberator." That's exactly the kind of joke Caroline would make. She said it sounded like an anecdote for *Reader's Digest* and suggested Mary write it up and send it in.

Imagine thinking Mary could do that. Patty was still with her every minute of the day, practically attached to her, holding her hem, or her leg, or her apron, her thin little arms always outstretched, begging to be picked up. Mary had practically pushed Patty out the door this morning. This was all her fault.

And she had a fourth on the way. The only person she had told was Caroline. She hadn't even told Dan yet. She had only just missed her period, but she knew. All the other signs were there. She was crying about everything. Every little thing. Caroline had hugged her close and then held her at arm's length by the shoulders, looked her right in the eyes and said, "How do you feel?" The question made Mary look away and tear up. "Oh dear," Caroline said, hugging her again. Caroline was a good listener, even when Mary didn't say anything at all.

An hour later, Patty had three stitches in her arm and was curled up in the Emergency waiting room chair beside Mary, sound asleep. The scar would not be any worse than the one left by her smallpox vaccination, the doctor said. Mary teared up anyway.

When they arrived back home, Dan was in the driveway. "Bud came over and told me. I was on my way to the hospital." He scooped Patty from Mary's arms.

Mary gave Caroline a hug and said, "Thanks again." She waited for Dan to say thanks too, but he was already carrying Patty into the house. "I'll get the boys," she said.

"Don't worry. I'll send them home."

Inside, Dan said, "You should have called me."

"Caroline was here. We managed."

"You should have called me," he repeated.

Caroline had started taking night classes at the newly opened University of Windsor. Art History and Sociology, whatever that was. She had tried to explain it, but Mary still wasn't sure she understood. One night after dinner when Mary was finishing the supper dishes and Dan was still sitting at the table, Dan wondered aloud why Bud would let Caroline do such a thing. "Waste of money," he said.

Mary kept her back to him. The blackness of the failed backyard rink held her attention. The grass would probably be dead in the spring. Dan said, "Well?"

She knew what she was supposed to do. She was supposed to agree. She was supposed to say that Caroline should be satisfied at home. After all, on Bud's management salary, Caroline had everything any woman could possibly want. New Frigidaire appliances, including an under-the-counter dishwasher, and the car, of course. But Mary couldn't play her part. A tightness came over her as a series of possibilities opened and slammed shut just as fast. What if she said she did not think it was a waste of money at all? What if she said she admired Caroline's ambition? Would he stomp out of the room? Disappear into the basement for an hour or for the evening?

Disappearing forever would be bad. Maybe she could get her old job back at the department store. How could she do it all? A job and the kids. This was crazy thinking. How would she ever explain that their marriage had ended over a fight about her neighbour taking night classes? It didn't make any sense. Dan was a good man—everyone thought so. Set in his ways, but a good father. A good provider. He gave Mary her money every week without fail and she could buy her groceries and incidentals without having to account for every purchase like some of the wives on Talbot Crescent had to do. Sure, her allowance was never quite enough, but it was almost enough.

Why split up over someone else's situation? The plate and dishtowel were still in her hands. Dan was waiting for a response. This fight wasn't worth having. Besides, what was wrong between them had nothing to do with Caroline. The real problem was that when Dan had criticized Caroline for going to the university, Mary had felt the walls close in around her. How could she ever explain that? She had hated school.

Dan had stood up and said, "Waste of money" again, and went to the living room to watch TV with the kids.

On Monday morning, Mary went over to Caroline's with Patty on her hip and a plate of her famous corn flake cookies.

"You didn't have to."

"I know."

They went to their usual places in the kitchen and Caroline set Patty up in front of the TV with a glass of milk and one of Mary's cookies. The theme song from *The Friendly Giant* followed her back to the kitchen.

"She seems to have forgotten the whole thing."

"That Forrester kid…"

Caroline took a deep drag of her cigarette and blew the smoke out. "Did you talk to his mother?"

"No. She's got enough trouble."

It was hard to keep secrets on Talbot Crescent. The kids ran in packs and everyone knew everyone else's business. The Bartletts on the corner slept in the nude according to their seven-year-old, Nancy. The Fleming kids kept getting lice. Lorna Harper's mother died and they couldn't afford to send her home to Halifax for the funeral. And then there was Mrs. Forrester, who no one called by her first name. She was standoffish, but Mary once saw her in the grocery store wearing dark glasses that couldn't hide the black eye beneath. Sometimes a secret was just something no one talked about.

Mary said, "Can I ask you something?"

"Sure."

"How does Bud feel about your classes?"

Caroline rolled her eyes and stretched her arms above her head with interlaced fingers. It was the kind of stretch a person might have just before getting out of bed. "He's not interested. I try to talk to him about the lectures and what we read and his eyes glaze over, probably just like mine do when he talks about the plant. Or hockey. You know how it is."

Mary had no idea how it was.

"Last night we got in an argument though. There's this kid in my class. A war resister."

"War resister?"

"Okay, draft dodger. But my sociology professor says it matters what words you use. 'War resister' is brave. 'Draft dodger' is cowardly. This kid is brave. He left everything he knows to stay out of the war. He's homesick. I think about our boys. What if we lived on the other side of the river? What if the situation was reversed? I hope some nice lady would help Brian out. Or Sean. Or Dustin."

"Well, they'll never be drafted."

Caroline ignored her. "Anyway, he's got no place to stay. He's sleeping in the library. He's hiding, of course, but one of these days he's going to be found out. I thought we could have him here but Bud won't do it."

"Maybe he just doesn't want a stranger in the house."

Caroline stubbed her cigarette out a little too hard. "Never mind."

Mary felt a flush rise from her chest and through her cheeks. Somehow, she had let Caroline down.

"I'd better get going." The closing theme of *The Friendly Giant* was playing.

At dinner that night, Mary was quiet while Dan talked about some changes at the plant. When he finally asked her what she did today, Patty piped up. "We took cookies to Mrs. Bremner."

Dan's eyebrow raised. He didn't need to say anything. Besides, she would have been annoyed if he criticized Caroline in front of the kids.

"Thank-you cookies. For her help on Saturday." She got up to clear the plates.

Sean said, "Wait, I'm not finished yet," and pushed a huge forkful of potatoes into his mouth.

Mary was about to chastise him for his bad manners but then Dan smiled and said, "That's my boy."

"Can we watch TV?" Both he and Dustin looked up at her and not Dan. Mary was the keeper of the TV.

"Sure. One show. Take your sister."

"I'm coming too," said Dan. "Bonanza is on."

Alone in the kitchen, Mary dried the last of the glasses. There was a hard rap at the front door and Dan got up to get it. Mary was sure it would be Caroline, but when she looked into the living room, she was surprised to see Mrs. Forrester.

"Come in, please." Mary untied her apron and smoothed her skirt. "Can I take your coat?"

"Thank you, but I'm not staying." Mrs. Forrester stood in the doorway. "I don't mean to trouble you," she said. "I should have come much sooner but only learned today about Patty."

The Forrester kid appeared from behind her.

"Kevin has come to apologize."

"I'm sure it was an accident."

"I'm really sorry," said Kevin, glancing in at Sean, Dustin and Patty. "I'm sorry, Patty."

Mrs. Forrester said, "Go home now, Kevin."

Mrs. Forrester was as thin as a knife-edge. Her wrist bones were sharp beneath the hem of her sleeve as she maneuvered Kevin out of the doorway.

Gunfire rang from the TV.

"Well, I thought you would like to know that his foolishness got him the belt. He won't do it again."

Mary remembered Mrs. Forrester's black eye and wondered what Mrs. Forrester would never do again. She steadied herself against the doorframe. "That really wasn't necessary," she said. Tears sprang into her eyes and Mrs. Forrester noticed.

"I know what's necessary with my boy," she said.

"I didn't mean…" she hesitated. Dan took a step closer to her. A tear rolled down her cheek and she swept it away.

Dan stepped in. "Thanks for coming over. We appreciate it."

Mrs. Forrester nodded, turned, and left.

Dan closed the door behind her.

Mary shook her head and whispered, "That poor kid. Sean, invite him over after school one day this week."

"Who, Kevin?"

"Yes. Kevin."

"You've got to be kidding," said Dan.

"I'm not kidding."

Sean shrugged.

Gunshots rang out from the TV again. Mary cringed. "Isn't there anything else on?"

What is a baby?
Rona Altrows

IT WAS ASTONISHING to me that I had a baby at all. If in the previous year, 1974, someone had asked me, "What is a baby?" I might not have had an answer. When it came to other people's babies, I had never been a gusher. I had not babysat in my teens, except for one horrible misadventure when I'd had to call my mother in for help. So why a baby *now*, me single, in my mid-twenties, and in first-year law at McGill?

Well, it was an accident, a mechanical breakdown. Not even the best birth control methods are one hundred percent effective. That three percent must come from somewhere.

But having discovered I was pregnant, I decided this was an opportunity and embraced it. The baby's father did not. In fact, he refused to admit responsibility unless I agreed to terminate the pregnancy. So we parted company.

In deep ignorance, I plunged into the prospect of motherhood, knowing that if I needed help, I could always count on my parents. They were both excited the baby was coming. They had always been there for me and I knew that, of course, they always would be.

As it turned out, I only thought I knew.

Because, when I was seven months pregnant, my parents died tragically.

I missed them fiercely, had nightly dreams of confusion about whether they were alive or dead. Experienced crazy frustration that they had missed meeting the baby by just two months. But never once regretted my decision to have the baby, to raise the baby.

The baby was born. *What is a baby?* I asked myself. I still didn't have much of an idea. Is a baby someone who produces yellow poop, the colour and consistency of scrambled eggs? Is a baby someone prone to eczema, including broken skin, someone who can therefore wear cloth diapers only, and must have a gooey white paste spread over her tiny burning bum at every change? Is a baby someone who can't settle at night, who cries constantly and in full voice between eleven at night and four in the morning, due to an abdominal pain condition called "midnight colic"?

The baby was a free spirit. The maternity ward nurses had told me to swaddle her in a blanket. The baby would have none of it, insisted on full freedom of movement for all limbs at all times. From the first she hated having her hair washed. Then she developed cradle cap, which made her look like a feral kitten with dandruff, so I didn't like washing her hair either. Fine with her.

My house was chaotic. I'd always been a lousy housekeeper but now I was atrocious. I just didn't have time. The clutter was beyond belief. Laundry piled up, to the point that I dedicated a whole room to it and closed the door. Between single parenting, the demands of first-year law school, and lack of sleep, I was as big a mess as the house.

One morning when the baby was three months old, I put her on her back on the changing table, as usual. I had just removed her soiled diaper, cleaned her bum, and slathered on the gloppy zinc oxide cream. I reached over to pick up a fresh diaper from the pile I kept in a laundry basket next to the table, and as I did so, the baby, who had not yet learned to roll over, *did* roll over and dropped to the floor, landing on her head with a loud clunk. She was as startled as I—there was a moment of silence and then she let out a shattering scream. She cried and cried and I phoned a taxi, which arrived quickly, and off we sped to the Montreal Children's Hospital. On the way the baby stopped crying and switched to a giggle, which confused me. What the hell was so funny? Her mother had nearly cracked her head open. She could be brain-damaged, a victim of parental neglect. But the baby just continued to laugh. By the time the cab reached the hospital, I was torn between alarm and relief. The triage nurse asked me if the baby had lost consciousness at any point. *No.* Had she thrown up? *No.* Good, the nurse said, that's very good. The baby was seen quickly. Clearly at this hospital they took head injuries to heart. They plunked a headcover on her that made her look like a space alien in a cheesy sci-fi movie—a bathing cap with holes in it and electrodes sticking out of those holes. Then it was I who laughed. Maybe she was on the way to a life of misery but she looked ridiculous.

It was established that her brain function was normal and, also, she did not have a concussion. I was told to follow up with her nurse practitioner the next day, which I did.

She declared the baby to be in good shape. I told her I felt awful about the accident. Irresponsible. She said babies are always surprising their parents and what happened to the baby and me, or something similar, had happened to an uncountable number of other families. She said the fact my baby had rolled over at such a young age meant that she was ahead of most babies in her physical development. I was proud of the baby's athleticism but not of my parenting.

The next big challenge occurred when, at a year old, the baby got sick at daycare, began to run a high fever, and the daycare staff couldn't reach me, although they tried repeatedly all day. When I went to pick her up she was sleepy and her face was so flushed I was frightened. I brought her directly to the Children's, where they diagnosed her with pneumonia, prescribed penicillin, told me to give her acetaminophen every four hours and regular plain-water sponge baths, until the fever broke. They'd prefer to admit her, they said, but couldn't— there'd been an outbreak of pneumonia among babies and they did not have a bed for her. So. Home we were to go. Fear for the baby overtook me. I needed the Emerg doctor to help me get things into perspective.

"At least it's not life-threatening," I said.

"I'm afraid it is," he said.

He told me I would have to take shifts with my husband, sit up with the baby until the fever broke.

Well, there was no husband, or anyone else to share the job of making sure the baby didn't die, so I went home with her, to stay awake all night and beyond if necessary. I was tired as well as terrified. Despite the fear, fatigue threatened to put me to sleep, so I drank many cups of coffee. Caffeine and adrenaline did the job. I stuck it out. In mid-morning, the fever broke. I called the director of the daycare to let her know the baby would make it. Then I got details from her about what had happened. Daycare staff had called the Faculty of Law nine times over four hours, in the hope they could get past the secretary who obstructed them. Each time they had explained that they had a very sick baby there who needed to be picked up by her mother. The daycare baby room teacher called, then the assistant director, then the director. The law school receptionist was adamant: I could not be pulled out of class. Class attendance was critical for all law students. Regular class attendance. Daily class attendance. She would not budge.

As I cared for the baby at home, I arranged for classmates to lend me their notes on the many lectures I was missing. When the baby slept, I studied. Once she was on the mend I called the dean's office and asked for an appointment. Who was I?, his secretary asked. I explained that I was a first-year student.

"Impossible," she said. "The dean is tied up all day."

"But it concerns the safety of my child," I said. "Surely he can take a few minutes."

She would not be swayed.

I asked my best friend to come over for a couple of hours and watch the baby. When he arrived, I got dressed as though I were going to a job interview, headed to the law school, walked into the waiting room of the dean's office. Told his secretary I needed to see the dean urgently.

"Regarding what?"

"The safety of my child."

"He's very busy. You'll have to book an appointment for another day."

Through the glass door, I could see the dean sitting in his office, the sanctum sanctorum, and started walking toward it. My boldness surprised even me.

"You can have five minutes," the secretary called.

Then, I knew I had control. At least for that moment.

I walked in.

"Yes?" he said.

I described the situation as succinctly as I could, and with as little perceptible emotion as possible. It seemed to me that this was a man ill at ease with displays of intense feelings, and what I wanted was a specific result.

"What are you asking me for?" he said.

I was pleasantly surprised with his directness. Maybe he was cutting to the chase because he wanted me out of there. I didn't care about his motives, as long as he came through for me.

"I need to know this won't happen again. I need your assurance that I'll be pulled out of class if the daycare staff calls about my child."

"I can give you no such assurance," he said.

I couldn't believe it. I hadn't expected a display of empathy. But he was a lawyer—wasn't he worried about liability? In all sincerity, I said I did not understand. Couldn't he simply speak to the receptionist, direct her to handle calls from the daycare differently?

"Administrative services are not within my bailiwick," he said.

"Well then," I said. "In effect you are telling me I'll have to choose between law school and my baby."

He said nothing, revealed nothing new through body language. Sat ramrod straight, waiting for me to leave his office.

A couple of days later, the law school receptionist's supervisor called me. "The receptionist feels terrible that she blocked the calls from the daycare staff," she said.

I didn't care. A baby's life had been involved and the receptionist should have known better. But the supervisor did tell me nothing like this would happen again. Ever.

So the dean *had* talked to someone after all.

Maybe he did know what a baby was.

And by then, in my life as a parent, I did too.

All That History

Doris Charest

Mothering My Mother

Katherine Matiko

We hold our stories in our bodies
tend them like eggs
release them one
by one.

I'm mothering
my mother
pacing my steps to hers
seeing the world with her eyes.
When a story comes
she smiles
a memory unbidden
an egg of a story
nurtured and kept
for many years
like a welcomed child.

She releases her story
and I catch it
tend it in my body,
in the hollow place
inside.

I'm mothering
my mother
holding her soft hands
stopping often
to look at her world.
Her stories are buried so deep
they may never hatch,
trapped in a tangled nest
of a brain. She is a fragile shell
of herself, freed now
from the relentless passage

of stories, of children
and time.

I'm mothering
my mother
saying goodbye
but afraid to release her
to the world.

Stories spill from her eyes
as she grasps my hands,
then simply lets me go.

Mother by Lightning
Kathleen Wall

Tonight, lightning urgently flickers old
black and white films of fifties thunderstorms
watched from our front porch.
A circuit breaker for my mother's moods:
the largesse of weather. Against the rain
pulled taut between sated cloud and lean
horizon, against "rain coming down in sheets,"
her words project plaints
about blunt ends of lipsticks,
the quarantine of kitchens, the bitch she feels
when she opens another can of tomato soup, until a crack
overhead tingles in our toes and blows
open a smile: "Nitrogen. Look how green…"
Tonight's storm blows east, shimmering
like sheet lightning we used to watch
on late summer nights
of Manhattans and dinner dresses,
the porch screens barely blurring the line
between indoors and out, the tender safety
of parents, aunts, and uncles talking quietly,
in civilized velvet voices
sometimes of the unexpected
flashes of light, sometimes
of what the light recalls: battles at sea,
hail-ruined crops, the brain's own storms.
Joe McCarthy. HUAC. From across the street
comes the hiss of a sprinkler
renewing one urban lawn
after August drought.

Mother bridges farm and town, knows
about carrots rotting in wet fields
but suspects no communists hide
behind the carrot fronds.

The only smoker, she takes off her apron after serving
chips and cocktail wieners in cut glass dishes, sits
in a far corner, blowing her smoke out the screen.
From the stairs inside, I see self-sufficiency, glamour even,
in the manicure lit by her cigarette.

If I walk outside memory, step onto the lawn,
home in on the ember in her hands,
I might catch her in a single blow
of light from a spent flashbulb, or lightning's
instant. "Mother, descending a staircase," each step
a line in the breviary of light and the alphabet of years.
And then another. And another.

B: Bottles
Kathleen Wall

Yehudi guarded the bottles that began to appear in the basement
once my father had finished putting shelves in what had once
been the coal room. We bottled pears and peaches each August,
buying them by the peck at the farmer's market if the fruit tree
blossoms hadn't been hit by late frost drifting in from Lake
Michigan. She and I would sit under the elm tree in the back
yard in our Bellaire lawn chairs with their clamshell backs, flat
roasting pans of fruit and peels on our laps, our hands dripping
sweetly, a large bowl between us for the ready fruit

making summer's ripe scent
and the shadowed air beneath the tree
that stroked our skin with hints of autumn
almost as eternal as the seasons. Each February
a season's death sighed out
as we opened the last jar,
each August a homely, taut rebirth.
Without their peels the quarts of fruit
lost the weight Cezanne gave to his apples,
their curves glistening against the glass,
the pears translucent, the peaches still
wearing the blush of their skin.

In a darker corner she kept
half a dozen gallon jars once full
of thin, salty-sharp pickles
or my uncle's maple syrup.
One she filled with red anger that looked
like animal faces, but none you recognized,
irate eyes and muzzles suspended
in clouds of red tempera.
Blue fury filled a jar
with nothing but the blue
of invisible work, invisible desires,

her knowledge obediently
turned clear blue.
Occasionally she kicked one,
and I could smell it everywhere.

She bought slender bottles at flea markets:
each a lucid chrysalis that once held
vanilla or a cup of cream,
bitters or lime cordial or perfume,
bottles you'd cluster on a picnic table and put
a single poppy in each, then listen
to them clinking in the wind. She bought
small corks and paraffin, sealing within
the songs of frogs, the memory
of hoarfrost (already a memory of fog),
a two-step with her husband.

Small clay bottles held music.
You could unseal
a yellow one to hear "Estralita,"
a pale blue one to hear Thaïs's "Meditation."
Squat brown bottles held hymns,
while the tall slender bottle
that Mother painted with the waxing
and waning moons that shaped her moods
held *Moonlight Sonata*, Debussy's *Clair de Lune*.

D: Dementia
Kathleen Wall

Don't upset the apple cart

Dementia
pulls down the blinds
with the patience
of a stoned tyrant
who is mesmerized
by the marvel
of each
tiny
change
For a while my mother
can count
each slat
accurately
from bottom to top
top to bottom
Or she does a quick
estimate, noting
how much of the moon
the mid-morning sun
the fir tree across Tom Smith Road
whose bending and swaying
speaks to her of time and weather
has disappeared

Then gravity implodes, its shrapnel mangles a hip and wedges light years between my hand touching her and memories of me playing Bach or hemming a dirndl skirt. Words crack at their seams—the acrobat somersaults too high to catch his trapeze, and becomes a constellation. Names crackle with lightning so they glow with sound but not with history. Her father's friend Herman Neumeier has a name so mellifluous (one of her favourite words; not lost yet) that it attaches itself to her physiotherapist and to the one man in the nursing home who can fix things. Places could have been moved anywhere. Paris a two-hour flight or several years at the speed of light. What does Paris mean?

Top to bottom means nothing

It's the deliberate
slowness that frightens her
makes her words weep
into the earpiece of the phone
that they won't let her
talk to me
"Why?"

No one ever returns
breaks the wax seal on the report
complete with maps and timetables
as if this were an escape route
a diversion from ache and loneliness

or the minotaur's labyrinth.
There is no string long enough

Don't you contradict me!

E: Eagles
Kathleen Wall

Elbow Grease

At the outset, we navigate
through constant change:
the county bulldozing new roads
to Hardy Dam each year. Two oaks,
drawn closer over the years by growth
and deafness, lean into their secrets
and leave space for us on the road.

On foot we navigate
by the shadows flickering
through spring's frail green
onto the forest floor. We are drawn
inward, by the darker places. Then
by trillium and blood root,
by the bright splash of cowslip
edging a creek where Dad takes his bearings.
We could follow the creek to the river,
and turn right, but he gauges the angle
that leads us every year to their eyrie.

My father navigates.
My mother—not knowing
the fratricide soon to occur
or the parents' passive collusion—
speaks wonder: the eagles' imposing wingspan
as they circle grandly, blazons their success.
We witness this flight each year
as if they were our springtime Orrery:
eyrie and brood the bright unmoving sun,
my parents merely planetary, subject
to the clockwork chains of seasons and cycles.
I a mere moon.

There is a different clockwork
in my mother's visits: once each year
she witnesses their puny angry cries
as if voice and words need not rhyme
to defend their owner's fierce entreaty
or stark desires.

Exhale!

Lessons
Myrl Coulter

from your mother, you learned how

to hold a baby, change a diaper,
fold laundry, iron tea towels,
make an apron on a Singer sewing machine,
kick an uncooperative clothes dryer

sweep a kitchen floor,
scrub over-used bathrooms,
chase carpet dirt with a testy vacuum cleaner,
dust furniture without breaking the Doulton figurines

peel potatoes, make gravy, bake cookies,
clear a table, wash dishes,
soak a burnt pea pot in the sink overnight,
use a wooden spoon to discipline children without ever
making contact

stop a bleeding nose, apply mercurochrome to scraped knees,
extinguish flames on a small human leg using a damp rug
that happened to be hanging on the clothesline,
rush a wounded child to the hospital in a neighbour's car

break a window by shaking a rolled-up newspaper
at a barking dog or a departing husband

shave your armpits,
put rollers in your hair,
walk in high heels,
clench your teeth,
be angry for a long long time

sigh soft and loud,
smoke a cigarette alone,
spend your evenings waiting

hold your head high through it all

miss her for the rest of your life

Nestlings
Louisa Howerow

When we were infants, we pressed our noses
into our mother's bosom, rooted for nipples,
sucked and sucked, and when we slept,
we buried our faces between her breasts.
When we were ready for more than milk,
she said, "Kiss, kiss, eat, eat," pinned her lips
against ours, and her tongue pushed bananas,
soft carrots, chewed meat into our mouths.
When in later years she told stories of famine,
finding bloated bodies on the road, the putrid fish
she ate head and all, we sat at heaping plates,
and what we couldn't eat, she finished for us.
Maybe at this point we should have said,
"Mama, we love you," instead of, "Stop,"
except our words were cruder, except
she couldn't and we couldn't.

I Am Ready to Memorize Mother
Josephine LoRe

I am ready to memorize mother
that new hesitation in her voice
as she asks again if she's added salt
to the tubettini bubbling in the pot

every time I fly back and hold her
she has shrunken one size smaller
shed inches of assurance
lost pounds of fierceness

I am afraid to delete her voicemail
though she always says the same things
– how are the kids? wear a scarf
make some honey-lemon for that throat

as if I were still 12, 12 again
and she's surprised at the recipes
I recite to her from memory, expressions
she taught me when I was a child

Sicilian expressions like
un cè du senza tri
things happen in threes
like my sisters and me

when she has grown small enough
I will fold her up and tuck her
into my breast pocket
so that she can feel forevermore

the drumbeat of my heart

As Tumbled Over Rim[1]
Claudia Coutu Radmore

she would have loved

the mason bee that pulls nails out of walls

and videos of Monty Python's silly walk

she said *of course I know the sun doesn't rise or set*

and *of course the stars and sky are not above us*

her reasoning not scientific but based on chthonic evidence

we had long acknowledged her mind to be simply different

never saw our mother as new type of mineral

harder and more valuable than diamond

and we thought

we thought

she would last forever

---

[1] The title "As Tumbled over Rim" is from "As Kingfishers Catch Fire" in *Gerard Manley Hopkins: Poems and Prose*, ed. W.H. Gardner (New York: Penguin Classics, 1985), 51.

Community

Sabine Lecorre-Moore

wishes, all in vain
Cathie Borrie

the woman, pregnant and overlooked
entered the bed of wonder.
she knew that she couldn't get anyone to love her
but her craving to be satisfied terrified her
and had become dangerous to deny.
in fear, the woman locked herself
inside a despair of words and misery.
in time, she gave birth to banishment
and was lost forever.

Bring Me Out in the Woods
Heidi Grogan

ANNA BEGGED ME, and I often obliged, because she was only five and I was already nine. In the dark when we couldn't sleep I told her fairy tales in a whisper.

All the stories began "Once there was…" The stories were always about justice. They moved from danger to happiness. They were about an orderly world where the children knew what would happen next. Where the children were rewarded, celebrated at great feasts, for being brave and doing the right thing.

Today I still crave that orderly world, one where I will know what's going to happen, one where brave girls are rewarded, where the good will be celebrated.

Back then, in the fairy tales I told Anna, there was always terrible punishment for the wicked. And all that had been taken was returned. Those who were dead were brought back to life.

Even as an adult now, I want this to be true. Especially in the tales I tell myself, and always in the ones that make me ravenous. The ones that bring me to joy, that bring me out in the woods.

Wolf's hunger gnaws, consuming her from the inside out— her own fine tissues—in a fierce contracting. In a war against an invasion of shadow. Gnaws and grinds the folds of her empty abdomen, and she winces from its twisting, from shadow and light battling there.

There is a wound on Wolf's withered haunch, festering since youth and stinking like sick, a putrid infection, provoking the iron-like old blood taste when the healing won't come. Her wound insists she limp, and splits Wolf wide in her walking: a wet and tender scar leaking pus, like sap from a tree, recalling its capacity for generosity. She remembers standing proud and productive. But that was before.

Now, she lifts her weight, holds her wasted, shrunken limb, this light limb, above the snow's crust, and her eyes gleam relief. The coarse bristling of her spine signals her soul's sight. On this night of many stars, a brilliant orb of a moon casts shadows onto her trail; she hobbles to her high place above the woods and is still.

Wolf is full of knowing: believes her wound is incurable. And in this place, she hangs her head low, then lifts, and cries her pain and her prayer, until her fierce worship of life force releases in a whimper.

The sun's orange glow will soon stretch itself across the treetops and into this frosted morning, promising warmth later in the day.

Morning will melt into deep snow, thaw earth, under which sleeps thistle, poppy, timothy and dandelion warmed by molten core. Dormant for perennial-pushing. *Later*, she thinks. *Maybe*. First, she must strengthen her spirit. And she knows promises bloom brightest after a necessary darkness. After times of cold.

Wild Rabbit crouches flat and frail, signs of grey betraying her pelt's white on snow, like low-weather wisps of clouds thickening, socking in. The grey tells on her, a cruel sabotage of time, or just necessity's bad timing. This work—adapting, avoiding predators, making home, home for sightless bunnies, it requires too much—productivity, activity, doing all that needs doing, perfectly and exactly. Her pelt is getting dull and worn thin she thinks, from the power-shifting seasons that dictate her changing colours.

Rabbit found clumps of faded fur in her tight burrow all winter, and she is cold. There, underground, walls and roots squeeze her space and she breathes shallow her own loneliness, her longing for a soul-home a barely beating desire.

Up here above ground, her racing pulse is focused solely on negotiating life. The survival strategy is also her lament: few notice Rabbit—her coat blending in for function. She lifts her hind leg, rubs paw on cheek for self-solace. Her own soft touch. She seeks nourishment, she seeks comfort, salve for the long disappointment of winter.

In these woods, Wolf whimpers. Rabbit flinches. On whom does the shadow rest, weighty and pushing into wound, below skin, melting into snow—Wolf or Rabbit? Whose blood will spill?

Wounded hungry Wolf chases down lonely Rabbit; limp dismissed in the running and wound seeping into matted fur.

For bolting Rabbit, the thrill of being recognized is momentary, and fear presses her forward. Fleeing hind legs snap snow back.

Wolf snarls into the flying ice. Frozen shards fly, disappear into the dawn's dark edges. Wolf's canines snap and grip, yellow on white, yellow on grey.

As the blood runs hard and warm, Rabbit spins to face Wolf. Shivers a faint rippling of fur over muscles. Holds eye contact, holds the amber eye of She-Wolf in her liquid blue, and trembles. Then she stays so, so still. Her only movement the twitching of her nose, allowing more air into her screaming lungs.

Wolf sits back on her haunches, cocks her head to the side, both ears perk forward. Wonders, has she been fooled out of her hunger, or if she should trust the prey, trust the wound. Before she can know the difference, Wolf and Rabbit jolt as one, a synchronized turning at a sound, a wail piercing the silence. Wolf's ears lie back, hard, for she is able to hear the highest pitches, and Rabbit's heart pounds, hard, for she knows pain when she hears it.

Here, around the grove of trees at the edge of the woods, is Woman. On all fours, and groaning. Guttural. Her bare feet are torn and bruised from the wood's branches. Dull hair, tangled and dirty, hides her face like a filthy curtain. She is near naked, gown half-undone at the front, revealing her losses. Her body is pasty and there is naught but a shadow where her blue-veined breast should hang above the diamond lit snow. Fleshy thighs ripple when she moves her knees wider, ribs heave over her pregnant abdomen as she strains—purple scar-stripes on her chest reach for the bright red stretch marks across her belly, white cords inside red mark the force on her frame, her pelvis opening wide, pulling skin, stretching it over her body's blossoming.

Woman cries out.

Wolf and Rabbit edge closer, together.

Woman looks up between dark strands of hair but her eyes are milky, glazed over, unseeing. Her pushing and tearing is anguishing. Prey and Predator stand beside her suffering. Encouraging. In courage.

Wolf and Rabbit pant in unison; they hold their breath when pain chokes Woman's exhalation.

When she heaves again over the snow, Rabbit's eyes follow Wolf's to the red spatters of birth's brilliance.

They crave transition too. Of the death that is necessary for life. This, they understand. And so they move closer still. The pungent odour of the sacred presses upon their flesh.

When the placenta slides from Woman, soft and quivering, she faints. Blood rushes away from her and onto the ground, rich and bright. Wolf devours the placenta greedily. Then stops, just before the final slurp of wet red. Looks from beneath her wild, coarse eyelashes to Rabbit.

Rabbit waits. No wise lenses of eyelashes to shield her sight. Hopes a raw, unfiltered hope. Dares in a new way of being, one that expects and insists.

Wolf bristles at the new demand. She sucks in her breath so hard it hurts, starts to snarl. Then. Nudges the still warm placenta with her soft black nose, moves its rich goodness across the wild grass pushing through icy snow to Rabbit's pink.

They eat together in communion.

Rabbit sits tall, fur shining, ears high and piloerection-alert, the fifty million cells in her twitching nose sensing the vital vision.

Wolf stops for a moment, looks up, really sees and understands Rabbit, her sight sharpened by this sacred consuming.

And when the consuming is complete, Rabbit and Wolf settle into Woman, one on each side of her, their pelts coarse and soft tight to her flushed skin. Warming her.

Woman sleeps, finally still.

Wolf's and Rabbit's eyes meet over her white body, curled and camouflaged on winter's ending.

The sun lies across Woman's rising and falling chest, heating the rhythms of her breath, her new life-song. Lies across Wolf's tender wound, drying and healing. Lies across Rabbit's lamenting heart, inviting joy there.

In her fingers she grasps fists full of fur, coarse grey, softest white warmth pushing up between her knuckles. The snow melting between her and Wolf and Rabbit is soaked red.

Woman's milk leaks down her belly and the ground turns pink.

Wolf howls in the afternoon of the day, the wild soul-voice of desire, of longing and gratitude. The shadows are gone.

And I forever want to oblige. I want to tell Anna. I want to tell her in full light when both of us are awake. I want to speak to her from a place without shadow. I want her to know there is reward for being brave. I want to tell her this story. The fairy tale, which begins, "Once there was…" and ends when what had been taken was returned: in kind. I want her to know the story of Wolf and Rabbit and Woman.

I need her to understand the tale of when thistle and poppy, timothy and dandelion pushed up like newly made nipples from the dermis of a skin of snow: shadow-less and proud.

I hope she will see them as sacramental symbols of those who were almost dead, like me; strong Women who birth their way back to life; brave girls who go out into the woods.

I Seek
Adrienne Adams

I am seeking a feminine voice echoing
across golden ages of curves that is
fat and kind and round
with wisdom dripping off her rims
in dregs of toffee ground tears
a voice that squeals with the high edge of
masculinity stretched beyond its breaking point
to give birth and bleed salt
into my years of knowing
just how deep I am and you are.

I am seeking a voice
that is valued for its vulnerability
for the strength in its years of innocence
so that I can leap
with unburdened joy.

I am seeking a voice full of motherhood
not just for all children
but for all the burgeoning things living inside
my friends' hearts of hearts
so that we are nurtured in such a way
we know we are loved infinitely
and all-ways.

I am seeking a voice that breaks the very bonds of its
oppression by dissolving
like water and flowing over
everything that has tried
to quell it.
This voice is a phallus crying
to be engulfed in heated convulsions
of sticky tides
speaking cunt language softly

with the sagacity of love
one word
with so many meanings
sucking on the suckling of sprouting
until we bloom and die and return
again weakly   monthly   daily
howling at the moon which
moves the tides of our enslaving in a steady stream
of transformation.

I am seeking a feminine voice that howls
content to be heard and valued for nothing other
than what it is.

I am seeking a feminism that embraces the feminine
in a humanitarian hug of x and y
chromosomes jumbled to spell lgbtq
forwards and back again
until we all know finally and forever
that we all come from our mothers' mothers' hearts
down an unbroken chain of eternity
that is boundless and flows
with the very life of blood
the first
sacrament
we partake.

This is my body.
Eat.
Feast.
Devour!

Hospital Corners and Tuesdays
Kari Strutt

My relationship with bedsheets is perhaps longer and more storied than most people would consider normal.

I cannot tolerate an unmade bed. I can, even less, embrace a sloppily made bed. If you are going to going to make a bed, it ought to be made well.

I am deeply committed to the hospital corner. I am a devotee of a top sheet doubled back over the blanket to a length of one foot. One foot exactly.

The bedspread must be pulled crisply over properly squared pillows.

"A well-made bed is your morning gift to the person you will be at end of the day." That is something my mother said.

I am the child my mother made.

My sheets are starched. Stretched tight. Carefully measured.

They are bleached white. They are bacteria-free, and lemon fresh.

When the army took hold of my hand and let me into her sterile barracks I was more at home than I was at home.

I made money making beds.

Four bunk beds per room. Eight mattresses. I made them all. One dollar per bed.

Double money, on clean sheet day. Two bucks a bunk. One buck for stripping. And one buck for re-sheeting.

I spit-shine boots as well, but only on Sundays. It should be a day of rest, but resting makes me restless.

I also shine shoes on Wednesdays. Wednesday shines are panty-hose shines. I can explain the difference if you need to know the difference, but most people don't care.

Warrant Officer Gladstone asks me on a Wednesday if he could possibly get spit-shined more often than the others. He asks me if it would be possible to be shined on Tuesdays, Thursdays and Saturdays.

I try to explain that I only spit shine on Wednesdays. I try to tell him that too much polish undoes itself. Too much polish gets scabby. You can't polish scabby polish.

You have to strip it down to the leather.

The Warrant tells me he's willing to risk it, asks me to pick up his boots on Tuesday night, bring them back the next morning.

In my heart I know that Tuesday night is not about picking up boots.

I would rather make beds. I would rather shine boots.

I would rather practice hospital corners.

I would rather make his bed than lie in it, but there is that other mouth to feed.

Another mouth to feed.

Gestation
Jayme D. Tucker

MOTHERS ARE GODS in the eyes of their children. They are our world, our protectors, our teachers. Our mothers give us what we need to survive in the world.

But, we all eventually kill our gods when we realize they are not gods at all.

It is a cruel death, when you realize that your mother is as fallible, human, and unconsciously cruel as you are. That one day you might become your mother.

So: you take a pill every day or endure shots once a month.

You implant metal into your womb so that your body is no longer a home.

You buy a vibrator to deny any possibilities worming their way into your bed, or your heart.

You are watchful, vigilant, wary.

You fight, and you fight, and fight to gut yourself, to take charge of your fate and your body.

You give your eggs away, cut your tubes, and excise your womb; you make sure you will never have to bear the pain of being killed in your child's eyes. So you do not have to bear the burden of passing on parts of yourself to a new life that's barely opening its eyes and squalling at the indignity of existence.

The pain of living is too great to pass on to an innocent.

But something stirs inside you anyway.

So you hold your friends close and love them the way they want
to be loved.

You take care with their names, and their preferences.

She, her, they, them, he, him.
Friend, darling, love, cinnamon bun, hun, dude, wife.
Beth, James, Travis, Nathan, Opal, Autumn, Jane.

You give them the little magics in you: stir vanilla and cinnamon into
hot chocolate, whisper soft promises into sugar cookies. You carefully
wind spells for happiness and warmth into your knitting, strength
into the patches you sew onto their jeans.

You give them smiles and comfort and a hand up when
they are down.

You tell jokes, whisper encouragements, celebrate with them in the
ways you know how, and tell them it's going to be okay. Everything is
going to be okay.

Sometimes you let them go.

You love them the way you wanted to be loved. You feed them
and fight for them, facing down threats like a bear protecting her
cubs. You face neglectful families, insecurity, and malformed coping
mechanisms forged in the fires of their childhood. You face down
their fears and give them the unconditional support you wanted,
that you needed. You keep telling them that everything is going
to be okay.

One day you realize you have children. Without meaning to, you have
become a mother to your friends, your comrades, your coworkers.
They come to you for comfort and advice, for something sweet, for
an open ear.

But on the inside something still aches, and they are not
quite enough.

You sleep on one side of your queen bed. You tear up watching couples hold hands on the train. You are so lonely that your bones hurt. You drown your sorrow and find it merely comatose at the bottom of a bottle, and still, you feel a hole inside.

You hear the oral tales of the many mothers that came before you. Mothers of tears, of sighs, of disappointment. Mothers of darkness and deep cruelty, of forests and hunger. You read accounts and testimonies, and try to find answers to the yawning emptiness inside.

You love and love and love, trying to find a missing half, a mate, your person. You spend too much time on websites crafting correspondences that are not returned and still you are empty.

You chase your loneliness to the edge of the universe, to a secret place.

You look into mirrors of knowledge, into scrying pools. You watch flames dance, you throw stones in the air, hoping that when they land the answer will be spelled out.

You walk to the edge of the void and cry into it. All your life, you were told you would become a mother. You became a mother to your friends, to the partners you loved and lost, to the people passing on the periphery of your story. It is a cruel joke then that you still feel empty.

"WHO DO I TAKE CARE OF THEN?" you cry, throwing your frustration into the void of that secret place; you collapse. You are spent, empty and tired and numb.

You spend a thousand years gently sniffling at the edge of the universe.

Softly, surprisingly, the void answers, "yourself."

The Unfathomable Attraction of the Man Who Wants a Mother
Aritha van Herk

THE MOTHER QUESTION, ah, the mother question.

"Do you have children?"

"Are you a mother?"

"Why not?"

"Do you object to motherhood?"

"Why have you have rejected motherhood?"

Danger lurks everywhere, especially related to mothering. She knows this very well. She is nobody's mother and she regrets that lack not at all.

Offering her the compliment of telling her that she would have been a great mother only makes her raise her eyebrows in that "seriously?" look.

Offering her the backhanded compliment of telling her that she would have made a terrible mother and it's a good thing she isn't, doesn't change her mind. She cannot even bother to be offended.

She has no children, has deliberately chosen not to have children. She works with students every day; she has an interest in cultural activity, and she keeps a killer schedule. Children demand a step out of time that she will not countenance. She does not regret her choice and the freedom it has granted her, watching the endless demands of her friends' children, for money, for the latest devices, for transport to their clubs and sports events, activities that would fill the Day-Timer of a corporate president.

But she does ask one question more often than she would wish, and less rhetorically than inclination would suggest. Sometimes she asks it of students, sometimes acquaintances, sometimes her brothers, sometimes even friends or colleagues.

"Who was your mother last year?" Drop dead serious.

Or, more crisply, "Who was your mother yesterday?"

The answer she receives usually involves chuckling recognition on the part of the respondent that she is unwilling to take on the appointed role, that she refuses to perform the nurturing act that they have—subtly or not—requested. Good-humouredly, of course, but with serious resolve.

However.

Worse than immature students, retro brothers, or self-absorbed colleagues, to her mind, are men looking for a mother. Her senses are sharpened by time and exposure for a hint of mother-fetish, mother-fixation, mother-lust, mother-seeking men, that special category of needy male who wants to find a mother.

Perhaps because of her hyper-awareness of this inclination, she has toyed with framing a *vade mecum* for women who need to beware men who want mothers. There are too many such men. They say they want wives or lovers or friends, but they are looking for women who will take on the physical and emotional role of mothers: support, nourishment, applause, emotional backbone, and clean underwear.

She offers her advice without rancour, but with the long experience of noting the particular behaviour of this type.

The man who wants a mother lives at home. Or has lived at home—well after turning thirty. He is reluctant to leave home, he is what is known as a slow leaver, someone who will stand at the door making self-evident comments for half an hour after he's been handed his coat. He is perpetually late, and every appellation of tardy, unpunctual and dilatory applies to him.

The man who wants a mother has excuses for everything. He's not to blame for his failed career as a would-be musician or his various bankruptcies. Not his fault, but the result of his being taken advantage of by a vague set of circumstances beyond his control. An innocent bystander, he can't understand why his credit card debt piled higher and higher. He was a gifted guitarist, but he didn't have a good instrument or the time to practice and the strings hurt his fingers. He wanted to become an engineer, but he couldn't afford the tuition for that many years of university. He found a roommate, but the guy bailed at the last moment. He's not married because of that nasty woman who jilted him, or the other bitch who destroyed his dreams. Whether the affliction is unemployment or poor money management or delusions of talent, his situation is someone else's fault. He didn't get the project done because they didn't give him what he needed to complete the project, so how could he? His contract wasn't extended because he is smarter than his boss, and his boss doesn't like him, and besides, his boss gave his nephew his job and turfed him. It wasn't worthwhile working when Employment Insurance paid more than working as a clerk. He grumbles about the supervisors who supervise him, how other people aren't doing a good job, how he is under-appreciated, how working is a drag, how his talent isn't appreciated. Even more relevant, he could have gotten roles as an actor but the guy who did his headshot didn't show his facial range. There are no bootstraps on this man's boots, no get-up-and-go, no sense that he might have to learn how to change his sheets or cook vegetables. Prone to finger pointing and poor-me pouting, he is a victim, and he wants a mother to take his side, paint mercurochrome on his scrapes and sympathize unwaveringly, morning, noon and night.

The man who wants a mother sneers at SUITS. Suits are men who polish their shoes, and tuck their shirts into their pants, and wear a tie, and maybe they've gone to school and become lawyers and they're all assholes. Because they're SUITS. Despite queries about single- or double-breasted, notch or shawl lapels, patch versus jetted pockets, this imprecation has nothing to do with the fictional Harvey Specter or his impeccable style. Specter knows enough not to wear a belt with a waistcoat, and his signature line is, "Like it or not, people respond to how you're dressed." No, this man will refuse to tuck his shirts into his pants, because sloppy dress serves as his greatest act of rebellion. He doesn't have a clue what side-vents are or what they mean. As for James Bond, isn't that story about guns more than style? And when it comes to "shaken or stirred," he'll have good old rum and coke. He carries his bills in a money clip, but he never has more than a twenty. For all his embrace of "casual Saturdays" sartorial dishevelment, he can't pass a mirror without stopping to look, in a strange duality of narcissism. And when he is faced with a decision, he'll talk to himself in the mirror, pro and con.

The man who wants a mother is lost more than found, vaguely unhappy with his life and not sure where he's heading. He wants a mother to complain to, to reassure him that he's an unacknowledged genius, a potential wizard or master, a maven who just hasn't been discovered. Success is a matter of luck, and he's just been unlucky, so he buys lottery tickets, and dreams of being respected for winning.

The man who wants a mother is the boy in the basement. Surrounded by light-swords and GI Joe figures and joke cowbells, this man's greatest ambition is to win a glow in the dark yo-yo competition, with flex tricks and moves like rocking the baby. This is the man-child who collects toy statues of his progressive rock heroes, complete with miniature keyboards and wind-up-key sound effects. He seriously believes that he has a mysterious spirit animal, and that he could have been a magician. "Magic" is his favourite word and the one he will use to seduce any mother-woman convinced by its insinuation. Although what he wants most is a magician's assistant, willing to be sawn in half, a sidekick with a rabbit in a top hat. Who will also be his mother. Dubious taste is a matter of pride for him. He mounts on his walls paintings of skulls, which he is convinced are cool. From no angle do these images connect to the Stoic practice of Memento Mori. As for Stoicism, emotional resilience and its resistance to destructive behaviour are beyond his comprehension.

The man who wants a mother is adept at micro-aggressions. He tailgates on the freeway while complaining about other drivers, rattles ice-cubes in his glass, plays endlessly repetitive music louder and louder, saves the pull-tabs of pop cans, hoards magazines that he will someday go through for good ideas for his unwritten songs, piles up used postage stamps and empty take-out containers.

The man who wants a mother is a food greenhorn. He has a touchy relationship to vegetables, his spices confined to salt and pepper. He cannot decipher food labels. He encounters fish only deep-fried with chips. Yoghurt makes him nervous. He pulls a five-year-old's grimace at eggplant, he is fond of pickles and he prefers to eat with his hands. At buffets, he piles his plate high, with an extra helping of condiments, and he slathers the butter on his roll all at once. He will put the coffee pot with the metal ring in the microwave and stand in awe at the sparks that result. He will leave a pot of water on the boil while he goes and takes a shower. He will confess, "I can't really cook. My mother wouldn't let me into the kitchen." Here is the crux, the "my incompetence is someone else's fault" position. He's a man on the lookout for a mother. He may seem presentable, might even, for a limited period of time, perform attentiveness, but no cultivated woman can go out to dinner with him.

The man who wants a mother will exhibit injudicious emotions. He holds tight to the bars of his insecurity playpen. "I feel anxious," "I haven't been happy," "I need to be creative," "I'm tired of this," "I don't want—" which can be completed with various nouns. "I feel" is his favourite phrase, and it conveys little or no energy, all self-regard.

The man who wants a mother will misuse words, will struggle to express himself. He will repeat over and over, "I'm trying to articulate—" as if he were declaring that he wants to learn ballroom dancing. There is no conclusion, and he will never understand that articulate is a verb that requires an object. He claims to be a good mimic but knows only one language. His malapropisms are unintentional, puns or not. Neologisms baffle him and spoonerisms are a mystery. He uses obtuse and abstruse interchangeably. He honestly believes that some deity created women to listen to him, sympathize and fulfill his needs, and he wants to find the mother-woman who will put up with his baggage, its broken handles and out-of-date luggage tags.

The man who wants a mother yearns for sympathy. When it does not appear, he resorts to an unembellished pout. He plays that walk-on role, imitating the cry of a cranky baby, and literally putting his thumb in his mouth in a queasily repellent gesture that is not funny at all.

The man who wants a mother will choose inappropriate moments to propose to women. Jokingly or not, especially when he is injured, he's on the lookout for someone to ease his pain, bandage the paper cuts. Having fallen and gashed his head, sitting in emergency, he will ask the nurse, "Will you marry me?" Having sprained his ankle, he will hint to the woman doctor, with only mild disingenuousness, that he is looking for a wife. When he gets a head cold and is recommended a decongestant, he will ask the pharmacist if she is married. He asks women to marry him when they exhibit attention to his needs, cook him breakfast, launder his socks or sympathize with how the world has done him wrong. He will fling himself down on his knees, of course, prone to dramatic gestures that draw attention, but this is only in order to attract a woman who will get him out of incipient difficulties, which might or might not involve police officers or traffic tickets.

The man who wants a mother claims that all his failures are because he fell for women who wanted too much. The word feminist throws him into a panic. His relationships have been tragic, although he will admit that he stayed longest with a woman because he loved her dog, and all he has really wanted all his life is a dog, while his first relationship and his last are with himself.

The man who wants a mother won't be found in the 'Diagnostic and Statistical Manual of Mental Disorders.' He exhibits just enough neurotic, narcissistic and selfish behaviour to slide onto the margins, dance on the edges of diagnosis, although mere labels cannot carry the dead weight, the bones and skin and blood of this man-child in search of a mother. Closed book or open, he's on to women who will put up with his junk and his hoarding, his narcissism and negativity. Avoiding him is another catechism entirely. And there are women who will laugh at his silliness as if it were a talent. Until it's time to remove him, like a plantar wart.

The man who wants a mother has a to-do list that will never be done. The kitchenette will never be tidy. The guitar will never be played. The shirt will never be ironed. The cupboards will always be jumbled with aging toffee and take-out containers. The freezer stacked with stale pumpkin pie will coat itself with un-defrosted ice.

But that doesn't take the cake.

In Margaret Atwood's novel *The Edible Woman*, the main character, Marian, bakes a cake-woman for the man who wants to devour her. And so, decisively and conclusively, the woman who is nobody's mother has one other piece of advice, good-humoured of course, although meant to be delivered with serious resolve: *offer the men who want a mother a version of that cake.* Because that is what they really want: to have their cake and eat it.

one moment of happiness
Cathie Borrie

lord have mercy on mothers.
in the wide world of sad and tired
they just want to die from sleep.

what do you want to die from? the quiet, hollow life?
or make mouths water, change silence into speak,
thirst into water, and bed a romp of brothers?

one day a beauty of mothers births an endowment
of secret words: *my child my child there's no more time.*

mother? mother?

Left Me Open
Natalie Meisner

How much meaning
can one word hold,
mother one mouth one
one wound one womb

Not a new question
to be sure
and I don't want to upset
the apple cart here
surely not toss the baby
with the bath
water broken are we
and healed by departures
and arrivals
like the gate of most fraught living flesh

As a queer woman
the word mother terrified me
so sure was I
the route was closed yet overdetermined
impossible yet defining but:
      somebody left me open
my first formed thought
when my son finally passed through
after a night of earthy animal horror
I won't traumatize you with here

All terror films, all war movies,
all knife wielding maniacs,
all visions of the violated body pale
under the bona fide pressure to declare all this
normal (It's not normal)
It's monstrous!

But luckily monstrosity
has its own power & beauty

& I'm not trying for redefinition
here mama mother mater mommy
we all have the right to
hunker down and heal
under the leafy verdant foliage
of any preverbal hum
from an infant mouth
that salves and soothes

I'm just making a few scratches
in the damp packed sand
of the shore that I was birthed on,
on the salty rim of the Atlantic
where low spruce
suck life from the rocky shoreline
and we are lapped by sea on two sides
tamped down by fog from above…

Where mother means the last
the only good thing you know
all that you lay down your life for
in the school yard
and ever since

Mother is the arm
that rises up
between you and harm
the candle ever aflame
in the harbour window
even when you, yourself
have given up hope of getting back onshore
The force bringing you home,
weaving to the door bashed up
drunk or sober

& what is mother now?
poised on the slicing edge of sacred & profane
she grows inside your brow
an emergent stone angel
you see surfacing in your own face
pushing up
through the bones of your own
from fathoms deep
through the good salt sea of milk

Is all tyranny infant tyranny?
The mothers seem to know
as they knit their brows
over cereal bowls
our worry the end of all happiness
our scream
a red ribbon in the wind
marking the beginning
the end of it all

Unrest
someone has left it open,
the gate is ever open
& you'll never sleep again

Who was it said
having a baby means
walking around with your heart
beating outside your skin
forever, mother

I can barely breath the word
Mother, so holy to me
though it may sound silly
to a culture used
to devouring you
without thanks
I don't care, mother

& I'll yell it from the mountain tops
if I live to see the day
that I'm half the mama
you were
& though I still don't feel worthy
of the mantle, mother
all I know is the gate is open,
Mama,
your smile warm butter in the pan
your scream the demarcation of time

You the first & the last,
the terrible & wonderful
one whose thankless task it will be
to plan our premature funerals
should we need them,
Oh, Mother
I know you would hurl the fist of dirt
on my grave
if that fork in the road
ever stuck itself in your eye

You the witness,
the gate,
& the light

Mama, you would bake a million files
into just as many prison cakes…
But this is my prayer, (me, who never prays)
My most earthy fervent wish:
Let us not make you
witness again and again
the indignity offered to our
bodies and spirits.

Ma, the sound warm smooth
the first ones made
on so many tongues…
you feed us and wipe our asses

Mother, you thrust yourself between me
& fate
between me and what meant
to devour me
"Not this one" you said. "No."
& showed me how to be human
that too

Where I come from
there are no women's shelters
no shelters for the mothers
they *are* the shelters for others
& who shelters them
is a thing that still keeps me
awake all night unblinking
in the dark just thinking:
something's not right

The gate's wide open
and swinging

Acknowledgements

(M)othering has been a labour of love, and we are grateful for those who believed in our vision and who came alongside to support its creation.

Profound thanks to everyone at Inanna Publications. Book making during a pandemic is incredibly difficult; how everyone at the press continued working with dedication and determination under such dire circumstances we are unsure, especially after the loss of Editor-in-Chief Luciana Ricciutelli (1958–2020). Brenda Cranney, Renée Knapp, and Ashley Rayner, your skill and professionalism speak to the reasons why Inanna is Canada's foremost feminist press.

When Luciana wrote us to say she'd like to publish this book, at the same time in her lovely way, she thanked us for sending *(M)othering* to Inanna. She understood how important the project was to us; we are honoured and deeply thankful for her belief in *(M)othering*.

Thank you to the editors Inanna assigned to work with us: Marlene Kadar (substantive editing) and Kimmy Beach (copy editing). We appreciate greatly your dedication to craft; we are grateful for your contributions to this book.

Anne Sorbie: I would like to thank Heidi Grogan: working together has been filled with deep exchanges and learning, with the kind of warmth, kindness and compassion that is so rare. To Rona Altrows, many, many thanks for your insight! You know intimately the joys and the challenges of curating an anthology. To dear friends and mentors who listened and walked with me along the way, my heartfelt thanks; you know who you are! To family. To my daughters Kim Budziak and Stacey Walz, and to my partner and husband Bob Hallett, thank you for your love and support of my work. You are always there, no matter what. My deep love and respect to the woman who was my mother: Anne Maria Sorbie (Moran).

Heidi Grogan: To work on a project such as this with a friend such as Anne has been a gift. To my husband Mike, and to our children Aidan and Abby, thank you for your encouragement and love, and for supporting the "othering" that is integral to mothering and writing. I also want to thank the birth mothers in my life for their grace and example of loving. A special thank you to my friends from Servants Anonymous Society of Calgary (now RESET) who showed me the ways community itself, in its vulnerability and in its strength, mothers. To my mother, and to all the mothers, grandmothers and mentors who were generous with their teachings, I am grateful.

From the heart, we'd like to thank those who trusted us with their stories and whose work we could not include in the book.

We were supported by two publications that anticipated the release of *(M)othering*. We wish to thank the Writers' Guild of Alberta and *WestWord* magazine for inviting us to write about anthology making and for publishing our article "Birthing Truths into the World" (Fall 2020). We also want to thank Darcie Friesen Hossack, editor at *WordCity Literary Journal*, for choosing "Mothering" as the May 2021 theme.

Finally, huge thanks to the writers and artists whose voices make these pages sing! We are absolutely honoured to be in your company.

Contributors

Adrienne Adams is a poet, artist and curator dedicated to creating safer inter-sectional space to honour the feminine. She curates Woolf's Voices,[1] joking that it's an excuse to howl in public. Her work is published in *Antilang*, *FreeFall*, *Politics/letters live* (Car Poems), *Polyglot*, *Wax Poetry and Art*, *Rose Quartz* and forthcoming in *NōD*, *Voices of Eve* and several other publications. Adrienne has featured at South Country Fair, The New Beat, The Storytellers (IndieYYC), Expressions Poetry, FlyWheel, University of Calgary Spoken Word, YYCSPEAK Reading Series, The People's Poetry and Ignite Festival. She has also co-curated for Single Onion and the Calgary International Spoken Word Festival. https://www.adrienneadamsartandpoetry.com

Rona Altrows is an essayist, fiction writer, editor and playwright. She is the author of three books of short fiction, *A Run on Hose*, *Key in Lock* and *At This Juncture*, and the children's book *The River Throws a Tantrum*. She has co-edited two anthologies, *Shy*, with Naomi K. Lewis, and *Waiting*, with Julie Sedivy. Her ten-minute plays have been produced in Canada and the United States. Her honours include the Jon Whyte Memorial Essay Award and The City of Calgary W.O. Mitchell Book Prize. http://www.ronaaltrows.com/

Ambivalently Yours is a Canadian artist who makes work inspired by her ambivalence, feminist questions and online interactions. Her aim is to highlight the potential for political resistance and emotional empathy that exists within conflicting emotions. Her work has been exhibited locally and internationally, shared virally on the Internet and featured prominently in online media publications, teenage blogs and zines worldwide. https://www.ambivalentlyyours.com/

Michelle Austen is a fervent plein-air painter who works and teaches in Calgary. She creates landscapes and florals, abstracts and whimsicals that reflect her untiring passion for colourful and exciting expressions in oil, watercolour and acrylic. For Michelle, a successful piece is one in which energy and life flow. Her artistic experience is grounded in over twenty years

---

[1] Woolf's Voices was founded on August 18, 2013, by Adrienne Adams to create a safe space for feminine identified individuals to present and celebrate work honouring the feminine—however they define that. It is a quarterly community event featuring poets, spoken word artists, musicians, writers, storytellers, etc.

of study locally and overseas. Michelle's work has been featured in numerous solo exhibitions, and in the Ranchmen's Club Annual Emerging Artist Event, the Calgary Stampede Annual Western Showcase and the Leighton Art Centre. Recently, Michelle's work was accepted into Calgary's Masters Gallery. https://michelleausten.ca/

Dorothy Bentley began writing poetry as a child. While she is previously published in non-fiction articles, columns and books, her poetry picture book *Summer North Coming*, was published in 2019, and a children's chapbook is forthcoming, both by Fitzhenry & Whiteside. Additionally, she studied literature and writing to earn a Bachelor of Arts in English, and works for the Writers' Guild of Alberta, southern Alberta office in Calgary. https://dorothybentley.ca

Sandy Bezanson holds a degree from Queen's University and has lived in a variety of overseas locations. Those experiences allowed her to pursue her love of art, history, peoples and place. She feels making these connections aided her subsequent teaching career, as did being a mother. Sandy returned to North America with a desire to write, and recently found the kind of bravery she needed to share her story, *Breathe.* Sandy's first book, a historical novel called *The Guernsey Diplomat*, will be published in 2022 by Friesen Press.

Cathie Borrie trained as a nurse in Vancouver and holds a Master of Public Health from Johns Hopkins University. She graduated from the University of Saskatchewan with a degree in law and has a Certificate in Creative Writing from Simon Fraser University. She lives in North Vancouver. Her memoir, *The Long Hello*, is published in Canada with Simon & Schuster and with Arcade (Skyhorse) in the United States.

Jennifer Carr lives in Santa Fe, New Mexico, with her partner and two children. She is an EMT, firefighter, author and poet. When she is not working at the local hospital or firehouse, she spends way too much time reading and writing poetry. Her poetry has been published in print and in online publications. Jennifer loves flying by her own wings and looks for any opportunity to soar to new heights. Follow her on Twitter @PoetryHaiku13. Jennifer can also be found on Facebook as Jennifer Carr Munoz. https://thebeautifulstuff.blog/tag/jennifer-carr-munoz/

Jane Cawthorne co-edited the anthologies *Impact: Women Writing After Concussion* (University of Alberta Press, 2021) and *Writing Menopause* (Inanna Publications, 2017), with E. D. Morin. Her first novel, *Patterson House*, is forthcoming with Inanna Publications. Her play *The Abortion Monologues* has been produced numerous times in Canada and the United States and is currently being made into an audiobook. Jane writes about women in times of transformation. https://janecawthorne.com/

Doris Charest's painting is a passion that has engulfed her life. She loves exploring with textures, shapes and a more contemporary look. Her goal is capturing nature in a way that the camera cannot. She won the Sylvie Brabant award in 2011 for her work in the art community. In 2017, her work was featured in *Oh West Canada!* by Imago Mundi. She teaches workshops both online and in person. https://www.dorischarest.ca

Marie-Manon Corbeil is an expressionist abstract artist based in Calgary. She is represented by two galleries in California and one in Canada. She has devoted her craft to vivid acrylic paints, rich in texture and vibrant in tone, but also evocative and expressive. Always developing her skills, Marie-Manon is achieving recognition worldwide by studying with renowned international instructors. She has been participating in mentorship programs with Jean Pederson and Robert Burridge, who are internationally known artists. Marie-Manon is passionate about giving back to her community, with particular support dedicated to helping children affected with Foetal Alcohol Spectrum Disorder (FASD). https://mariemanon.com/

Myrl Coulter is the author of three published books, most recently, *The Left-Handed Dinner Party and Other Stories* (University of Alberta Press, 2017), a collection of connected short stories. Her second book, *A Year of Days* (UAP, 2015), won an IPPY (Independent Publisher Book Award) bronze medal and was an INDIEFAB[2] finalist. Myrl's first book, *The House with the Broken Two: A Birthmother Remembers* (Anvil Press, 2011), won the 2010 First Book Competition sponsored by The Writers Studio at Simon Fraser University and the 2011 Canadian Authors Association Exporting Alberta award. Myrl's work has been published in *Geist*, *WestWord*, *Avenue Magazine* and in numerous anthologies. https://myrlcoulter.com/

Joan Crate lives in Calgary, Alberta. She is the mother of three sons and one daughter; each of her children was born in a different decade. She is also the proud grandmother to two lovely girls. Joan has published two novels and

---

[2] INDIEFAB are independently published Book of the Year Awards, judged by a select group of librarians and booksellers from around the country.

three books of poetry. Her first novel, *Breathing Water* (NeWest Press, 1989), was shortlisted for the Commonwealth Book Award (Canada) and the Books in Canada First Novel Award. She is a recipient of the Bliss Carman Poetry Award and her last book of poetry, *SubUrban Legends* (Freehand Books, 2009), was awarded Book of the Year by the Writers' Guild of Alberta. Joan's novel *Black Apple* was published by Simon & Schuster in 2016 and won The City of Calgary W.O. Mitchell Book Prize in 2017.

Amy Dryer received her BA in Fine Arts via the Alberta College of Art and Design, the Glasgow School of Art and the Fine Art program at Mount Allison University. In 2008, she was on the cover of *Avenue* as "Calgary's Best" and was featured again in their 2016 "Top 40 Under 40" issue. She's completed artist residencies in Canada, Iceland and Germany. Her paintings are in collections throughout Canada and the United States. Amy's German Expressionism gestural style emphasizes the subjective expression of inner experiences. The truest picture of a moment—the figure of a place—occurs in a balanced abstraction of everyday perspectives. http://www.fragmentsofsoul.com/

Daniela Elza's poetry collections are *the weight of dew* (Mother Tongue Publishing, 2012), *the book of it* (iCrow Publications, 2011) and *milk tooth bane bone* (Leaf Press, 2013). Her poems have won numerous contests and have been nominated for the Pushcart Prize and *Best of the Net* anthology multiple times. Her essay "Bringing the Roots Home" was nominated for the 2018 Pushcart Prize. Born and bred between three continents, Daniela is used to crossing borders and dwelling in liminal, and in-between spaces. Her latest book, *the broken boat*, from Mother Tongue Publishing, launched in April 2020.

Sanita Fejzić is an award-winning Bosnian-Canadian writer. Fejzić has published her poetry and short stories in literary magazines across Canada. Her poem "(M)other" was shortlisted for the CBC Poetry Prize. A children's book version of "(M)other" was translated into French by Sylvie Nicolas as "Mère(s) et monde" and illustrated by Alisa Arsenaud. Fejzić is also a novelist, playwright and scholar. She lives in Ottawa with her wife and two children.

Melanie Flores is Toronto-born and she divides her time between working as an editor/writer and writing poetry and short prose. Melanie has been a contest winner in several poetry competitions, including a first place award for "Final Moments" in the Polar Expressions Publishing's 2017 National Poetry Contest. Melanie's poetry has appeared in *Fresh Voices, FemCaucus*

Newsletter, The Prairie Journal, Dancing on Stones anthology and in *Universal Oneness: An Anthology of Magnum Opus Poems.* Her work is slated to appear in upcoming national and international anthologies. An Associate Member of the League of Canadian Poets, Melanie self-published her first chapbook, *The She: An Exposé*, in the summer of 2019.

Darcie Friesen Hossack is the author of *Mennonites Don't Dance* (Thistledown Press, 2010). The book was a finalist for the Danuta Gleed Literary Award and was shortlisted for the Commonwealth Writers' Prize (Canada and the Caribbean). She is a food writer and photographer, a three-time judge of the Whistler Independent Book Awards and is completing a novel that introduces the odd realities of her Mennonite and Seventh-day Adventist upbringing. Darcie currently lives near Jasper, Alberta, with her chef husband and their two fully conversational Oriental Shorthair cats.

Jessica Gigot is a poet, farmer, teacher and musician. She has a small farm in Bow, Washington, called Harmony Fields that makes artisan sheep cheese and grows organic herbs. Her first book of poems, *Flood Patterns*, was published by Antrim House Books in 2015. Her writing appears in several publications, including *Orion, Gastronomica, Taproot, The Hopper* and *Poetry Northwest*.

Heidi Grogan's writing and work address issues at the intersection of trauma, social justice and spirituality. She has published in *ROOM* magazine, *Weavings* and the *Boobs* anthology (Caitlin Press, 2016). Her love for teaching creative writing has seen her offering courses at Calgary universities, and for fifteen years she facilitated creative writing classes for women healing from sexual exploitation and edited their publication, *Cry of the Streets*. She has engaged adults healing from trauma in multiple Calgary programs, attending to the links between poverty, literacy and literary fluency. https://www. heidigrogan.ca/.

"Bring Me Out in the Woods" alludes to "The Wolf's Eyelash," cited by Clarissa Pinkola Estés in *Women Who Run with the Wolves: Myths and Stories of the Wild Woman Archetype.* New York: Ballantine Books, 1995.

Vivian Hansen has published poetry, creative non-fiction, essays and memoir in Canadian journals and anthologies. "Hundedagene and the Foxtail Phenomenon" was published in *Coming Here, Being Here* (Guernica Editions, 2016). "Telling" was published in *Waiting* (University of Alberta Press, 2018). Her three full-length books of poetry are *Leylines of My Flesh* (Touchwood Press, 2002), *A Bitter Mood of Clouds* and *A Tincture of Sunlight* (Frontenac House, 2013 and 2017). She published a long poem, "Design Charette for

Blakiston Park," with Loft 112 in 2019. Her contribution to *(M)othering*, "Toward Hygge," was published in *Freefall* XXVII, no. 1 (Winter 2018). Vivian teaches poetry and creative writing in Calgary.

Lisa Harris is a Pushcart Prize nominee who writes about growing up, outdoor adventure, science and coping with speed bumps. Her work has appeared in the *Boston Globe, Christian Science Monitor, Raleigh Review, Black Fox Literary Review* and *Highlights for Children.* She also co-authored an environmental policy book (ed. Krausman and Harris, *Cumulative Effects in Wildlife Management: Impact Mitigation.* Boca Raton: CRC Press, 2011). Lisa lives in Tucson with two daughters, four cats, nine desert tortoises, a scruffy terrier and a blind herding dog named Noel. She works as an environmental consultant and is in search of an agent for her latest novel. http://www. lisakharris.com

Elaine Hayes is a writer based in White Rock, BC. She studied creative writing at the University of Calgary and the Humber School for Writers, and was a recipient of an Alberta Foundation for the Arts Literary Arts Project Grant. Her work has appeared in numerous publications, including *grain, Writing Menopause* (Inanna Publications, 2017), *Alberta Views* and *Somebody's Child: Stories about Adoption* (TouchWood Editions, 2011). http://www. elainehayes.com

Barb Howard has published four novels and one short story collection. Her most recent novel is *Happy Sands*—published in 2021 by the University of Calgary Press. Barb's awards include the Howard O'Hagan Award for Short Story and the Canadian Authors Association Exporting Alberta Award. Her fiction and non-fiction have appeared in magazines, journals and anthologies across Canada. Barb is the Calgary writing mentor and national chair of The Shoe Project—a literacy and performance workshop for immigrant and refugee women. She is a past author-in-residence at the Calgary Public Library, a former editor of *Freefall* magazine, and an erstwhile creative writing instructor and mentor at various venues including the University of Calgary, The Banff Centre for Arts and Creativity and the Alexandra Writers' Centre. https://www.barbhoward.ca/.

"Bigfoot Therapy" was previously published in *Broken Pencil* online, November 21, 2017. https://brokenpencil.com/news/fiction-bogfoot-therapy

Louisa Howerow's poems have appeared in a number of anthologies, among them: *Gush: Menstrual Manifestos for Our Times* (Frontenac House, 2018), *Another Dysfunctional Cancer Poem Anthology* (Mansfield Press, 2018),

Resistance: Righteous Rage in the Age of #MeToo (University of Regina Press, 2020) and *GUEST* #19 (guest editor Pearl Pirie, above/ground press, 2019). Her poems "Why Scrabble" and "The Why of It" were selected for Poem in Your Pocket Day, 2020 and 2021 respectively.

Melanie Jones is an award-winning writer, performer and producer whose work has been called "bracing and beautiful ... absolutely intoxicating" by the *New York Times*. Jones has created six full-length theatre and performance works, including *ENDURE: A Run Woman Show*, which was a *New York Times* Critic's Pick and has toured internationally. She is the author of four published non-fiction books. She has written, produced and hosted more than fifty episodes for CityTV; fifty-five videos for BreathingRoom, an award-winning online resource for at-risk youth; and more than twenty-five stories for Waves of Change, documenting the world water crisis.

Kelly Kaur's poems and works have been published in *Anak Sastra*, *Time of the Poet Republic*, *Blindman Session Beer Cans*, *Best Asian Short Stories 2020*, *This Might Help*, *BeZine*, *Understorey* magazine and *International Human Rights Arts Festival*. Her novel, *Letters to Singapore*, will be published by Stonehouse Publishing in Spring 2022.

Norma Kerby has been published in journals, e-zines, magazines and anthologies, most recently in the anthologies *Heartwood* (League of Canadian Poets, 2018), *Another Dysfunctional Cancer Poem Anthology* (Mansfield Press, 2018), *Shadows and Light* (Writers North of 54, 2018) and *Somewhere My Love* (Subterranean Blue Poetry, 2018). As well, her chapbook *Shores of Haida Gwaii* was published in 2018 (Big Pond Rumours Press). Nominated for a Pushcart Prize in 2017 (*Prairie Journal*), she writes about environmental, ecological and social issues, in particular those affecting rural and northern Canada.

Shannon Kernaghan writes and creates visual art from Alberta. She enjoyed life as a "digital nomad" for years, travelling and writing from her RV. Her work appears in books and journals—poetry, fiction and everything between—and she continues to tell her stories at https://www.shannonkernaghan.com.

Liz Kingsley is a poet and the Administrative Director of The Writers Studio. She is a graduate of Mount Holyoke College and New York University. Her poetry has appeared or is forthcoming in *New Ohio Review*, *The McNeese Review*, *The Round Euphony*, *Exit 13* and *Tipping the Scales*, and her fiction has appeared in *The William and Mary Review*. Her personal essays have been published in *New Jersey Family* and the anthology *Blended: Writers on* *the Stepfamily Experience* (Seal Press, 2015). She received Pushcart Prize nominations in 2013, 2019 and 2021. She lives in New Jersey with her wife and eight children (five human, two canine, one feline).

Penney Kome is an award-winning journalist and the author of six non-fiction books. She has had two parents and three stepparents, one younger than her. Her siblings are even more complicated. Counting the children they have between them, her mother has three kids and her dad has six. Every brother has two brothers. One sister has one brother and one sister. Two sisters have two brothers and two sisters apiece, and one sister has three brothers and three sisters. How many children are there altogether? (Seven.)

Chynna Laird is a mother of four, a freelance writer, blogger, editor and award-winning author. Her passion is helping children and families living with Sensory Processing Disorder (SPD), mental and/or emotional struggles and other special needs. She has authored two children's books, two memoirs, a parent-to-parent resource book, a young adult novella, a young adult paranormal/suspense novel series, two new-adult contemporary novels and an adult suspense/thriller. http://www.chynnalairdauthor.ca/

Sabine Lecorre-Moore was born in 1970 in Montreal. Soon after, her parents returned to the French Alps, where she grew up. She attended high school in Annecy to study visual arts. In 1991, she obtained a diploma at the École supérieur de peinture Van Der Kelen-Logelain in Brussels. The same year, she moved to Calgary. During the next two decades, she realized many public and private decorative art projects. Since 2009, Sabine has dedicated herself entirely to her career as a professional artist. http://sabinelecorremoore.com/

Josephine LoRe's words have been read on stage and in Zoom rooms globally, published in eleven countries and three languages, put to music, danced and integrated into visual art. In 2021, her poetry was published in Canada's *FreeFall* and *Vallum* magazines, the *Fixed and Free Anthology* in the US (Mercury HeartLink), and Ireland's *Same Page Anthology*. Josephine has two collections, which integrate her poetry and photography: *Unity* and the *Calgary Herald* bestseller *The Cowichan Series* (Kouros Publications, 2019). She belongs and contributes to a variety of Canadian and international poetry societies. https://www.josephinelorepoet.com/

Patricia Lortie was born in Quebec where she studied Industrial Design and Business Administration. In 1995, she relocated to Calgary where she studied at the Alberta College of Art and Design. Her art practice covers painting, sculpture, installation, video, public art and arts education. She exhibits regularly in public and commercial galleries. She is co-founder of the collective DEVENIR, which includes five Francophone female artists from Alberta. She has served on arts organizations boards and committees such as the Arts Advisory Committee of the Alberta Legislative Assembly, the programing committee for the KOAC (Kiyooka Ohe Arts Center), the Board of Sava (Société des arts visuel de l'Alberta), and the Board of rafa (Regroupement Artistique Francophone de l'Alberta). https://patricialortie.com/

Kim Mannix is a poet, fiction writer and journalist from Sherwood Park, Alberta. She has been published in several journals and anthologies and is a co-editor of *Watch Your Head*, a climate crisis anthology (Coach House Books, 2020). She is the mother of two kids, and deeply grateful to the earth that sustains all of us. You can find her on Twitter @KimMannix posting about music, cats and spooky things.

Katherine Matiko contributed to the mission of many non-profit organizations during her career as a communications professional. They ranged from charities and post-secondary institutions to government and healthcare organizations. As she gratefully brings her working career to a close, she is finally focusing on her own writing. She is currently working on a short story collection, seeking inspiration from the seemingly unremarkable Calgary suburb where she has lived for the past twenty-two years.

Natalie Meisner is an award-winning multi-genre author and 5th Poet Laureate of Calgary. Her work deploys the power of comedy for social change. She is a wife and mom to two great boys and a full Professor in the Department of English at Mount Royal University where she works in the areas of creative writing, drama and gender/ sexuality studies. She has published six books: *Speed Dating For Sperm Donors*, *Baddie One Shoe*, *Legislating Love: The Everett Klippert Story*, *My Mommy, My Mama, My Brother & Me*, *Double Pregnant: Two Lesbians Make a Family* and *Growing Up Salty*. "Left Me Open" is published in *Baddie One Shoe* and is published here with the kind permission of Frontenac House. http://www.nataliemeisner.com

Michael is studying for a master's degree and has been published in various online platforms. His work in this anthology shares the kind of inter-generational trauma that is rarely spoken of; we commend his bravery.

E. D. Morin's writing has appeared in *You Look Good for Your Age* (ed. Rona Altrows, University of Alberta Press, 2021), *New Forum*, a Calgary women's arts and literature magazine, and other publications across North America. Her work has also aired on CBC Radio. With Jane Cawthorne, she is the editor of two anthologies: *Impact: Women Writing after Concussion* (University of Alberta Press, 2021) and *Writing Menopause* (Inanna Publications, 2017). She honours and acknowledges the beautiful land of Calgary/Mohkínstsis where she lives.

Kyle Nylund is an artist and educator currently residing in Vancouver, British Columbia. He has a Bachelor of Fine Art from the Alberta University of Art and Design and a Bachelor of Education from the University of British Columbia. His professional artistic practice deals with issues of sexual identity and belonging, and exploring the human condition through various mediums including paint, textiles and the performative arts.

Susan Ouriou is an award-winning fiction writer, editor and literary translator who has published a number of short stories as well as two novels, *Nathan* (Red Deer Press, 2016) and *Damselfish* (Dundurn Press, 2003), and numerous translations from Spanish and French. Susan is also a mother to two beloved daughters—Christelle, a teacher and mother herself, and Katie, whose life was cut short at the age of sixteen—and a grandmother to two other amazing human beings.

Julianne Palumbo is a mother, a writer and a writing encourager. She has published poems, short stories and essays, and continues to dream about publication of her YA novels-in-verse. She is the author of *Into Your Light* (Flutter Press, 2013), *Announcing the Thaw* (Finishing Line Press, 2014) and *50/50* (Unsolicited Press, 2018). She is the Founder/Editor of *Mothers Always Write*, an online literary magazine about motherhood, and the MAW Literary Writers Boot Camp. When she is not writing, you will find her in the kitchen or the garden or walking the dog.

Claudia Coutu Radmore is a Montreal-born writer who has taught and created art in Quebec, Ontario, Manitoba, China and Vanuatu. She is the President of Haiku Canada. *Accidentals* (Apt. 9 Press) won the 2011 bpNichol Chapbook Award; *On Fogo*, which was short-listed for the 2017 Malahat Long Poem Contest, was subsequently published by The Alfred Gustav Press, Vancouver, in 2018. Her poem "the breast for sappiness," first published in *filling Station*, was included in *The Best Canadian Poetry of 2019* (Biblioasis Press). Her latest collections, both published in 2020, are *rabbit* (Aeolus House Press), and *Park Ex Girl: Life with Gasometer* (Shoreline Press).

Lori D. Roadhouse is a Calgary poet and writer. She is a member of the Alexandra Writers' Centre Society and the Writers' Guild of Alberta. Since 2007 she has been on the board of the Single Onion Poetry Series. From 2008 to 2010 she was co-artistic director, performer and emcee of Lotus Land at South Country Fair and was the 2009 Poet-in-Residence for *Radiant Lights* eMagazine. Lori co-created the Writing Toward the Light Poetry Contest and Concert. Lori was the 2015 Poet Laureate for the PGI Literacy event with CanLearn Society. She is currently the consulting editor for *WordCity* Monthly. Recent publications include *Tap Press Read*, *YYC POP: Poetic Portraits of People* (ed. Sheri-D Wilson, Frontenac House, 2020) and *The Time of the Poet Republic*.

Joan Shillington is a Calgary poet who writes in a loft overlooking the Rocky Mountains. She has been published in *The Antigonish Review*, *grain*, *Prairie Fire*, *FreeFall*, *CV2* and has placed first, second and honourable mention in poetry contests. As well, she has poems in various anthologies. Her third collection of poetry, *Let This Lake Remember*, was published by Frontenac House in 2020.

Katherine Smart is a stay-at-home mom of two sweet daughters. Her children light up her world—sometimes with their adorable smiles and playful enthusiasm and other times with firecrackers strapped to the dog's back set off inches from her face at 3:00 a.m. She writes in her head all day long. Prior to parenting full-time, Katherine worked in fundraising and communications for Calgary's charitable sector.

Anne Sorbie's fiction, poetry, essays and book reviews have been published by Inanna Publications, the University of Alberta Press, Frontenac House, House of Blue Skies and Thistledown Press; in magazines and journals such as *Alberta Views*, *Geist* and *Other Voices*; and online with Brick Books, *CBC Canada Writes* and *Geist*. Anne's third book, *Falling Backwards into Mirrors*, was published by Inanna Publications in 2019. Most recently, her work can be found in the anthology *You Look Good for Your Age* (University of Alberta Press, 2021). She is a mother/stepmother of five and grandmother of three. https://www.annesorbie.com/

Kari Strutt lives, writes and walks her dogs in Calgary, Alberta. She is an apprentice woodworker, a collector of pinecones and a terrible cook. Her work has appeared in *grain*, *Prism*, *Room*, *Event* and in a high school textbook titled *Imprints 12*.

Kelly S. Thompson is a retired military officer who holds an MFA in Creative Writing from the University of British Columbia and is a PhD candidate at the University of Gloucestershire. She has won several writing awards, including the 2017 House of Anansi Press Golden Anniversary Short Story Contest, the 2014 and 2017 Barbara Novak Award for Personal Essay and second place in the 2019 *Room* Magazine Creative Non-Fiction Contest. Her essays have appeared in several anthologies and in publications such as *Globe and Mail*, *Chatelaine*, *Maclean's* and more. Her memoir, *Girls Need Not Apply*, was an instant *Globe and Mail* bestseller and rated one of their top 100 books of 2019. Her next memoir, based on her *(M)othering* essay will be released in 2023 with McClelland & Stewart. https://kellysthompson.com

Dr. Yvonne Trainer is a poet, editor, researcher and writer in Lethbridge, Alberta. She has published a chapbook and four books of poetry and is a member of the League of Canadian Poets and Academy of American Poets. Her First Nations poetry collection *Tom Three Persons* (Frontenac House, 2002) has been read both nationally and internationally. Recently, Yvonne's work has appeared in *YYC POP: Poetic Portraits of People* (ed. Sheri-D Wilson, Frontenac House, 2020), *Calgary Through the Eyes of Writers* (ed. Shaun Hunter, RMB, 2018) and in *WordCityLit* (ed. Darcie Friesen Hossack). More recent poems by Yvonne are available via the DogWood Reading Series on YouTube.

Jayme D. Tucker is a writer, streamer and performer settled on unceded Syilx territory, formerly an emcee and performer from Mohkintsis. They're queer, tall and very dramatic, so they do comedy onstage and online. They've written for www.thehub.lgbt Kelowna, and performed in the 2019 Femme Wave Festival as well as the 2020 Calgary Pride virtual festival. They are the founder of The Queer Agenda, a non-profit social group focused on sober friendly, all-ages networking for LGBTQ2IA+ individuals.

Aritha van Herk is nobody's mother, but she is the author of five novels, *Judith* (Bantam, 1979), *The Tent Peg* (Red Deer Press, 2005), *No Fixed Address* (Red Deer Press, 2002), *Places Far from Ellesmere* (Red Deer Press, 2003) and *Restlessness* (Red Deer Press, 2005), five works of non-fiction, most notably *Mavericks: An Incorrigible History of Alberta* (Penguin, 2001), and a work of prose-poetry, *Stampede and the Westness of West* (Frontenac House, 2016). She has published hundreds of stories, articles, reviews and essays on Canadian culture, material culture and women's experience. She is a Member of the Order of Canada and the Alberta Order of Excellence. She lives in Calgary, Canada. http://www.arithavanherk.com/

Katherena Vermette is a Métis writer from Treaty One territory in Winnipeg. Her first book, *North End Love Songs* (The Muses' Company, 2012), won the Governor General's Literary Award for Poetry. Her novel *The Break* (House of Anansi Press, 2016) was a bestseller in Canada and won multiple awards, including the 2017 Amazon.ca First Novel Award. *The Strangers* (Penguin Random House, 2021) is her most recent award-winning novel. Along with a team of talented filmmakers, she co-wrote and co-directed the short documentary *this river* (National Film Board), which won the 2017 Canadian Screen Award for Best Short Documentary. Vermette is always working on new stuff, and lives with her family in a cranky old house within skipping distance of the temperamental Red River.

Kathleen Wall is the author of three books of poetry, *Without Benefit of Words* (Turnstone Press, 1991), *Time's Body* (Hagios Press, 2005) and *Visible Cities* (University of Calgary Press, 2018), and of one novel, *Blue Duets* (Brindle and Glass Publishing, 2010). She is working on a second novel, *Soul Weather*, and on a fourth book of poems, tentatively titled *Aides Memoire*. The poems included here are a section of that work and are an abecedarius that explores both her mother's life and the experience of motherhood in the fifties and sixties. https://blueduets.blogspot.com

Poems by Kathleen Wall are excerpted from a series called "The Abecedarius," which in turn, is part of a larger project (in progress) on memory entitled *Aides Memoire*. "Bottles" was previously published in *CV2*, Summer 2020.

Mary Warren Foulk has been published in *VoiceCatcher*, *Hip Mama*, *Cathexis Northwest Press*, *Yes Poetry*, *Arlington Literary Journal* (Gival Press) and *Palette Poetry*, among other publications. Her work also has appeared in *Who's Your Mama?: The Unsung Voices of Women and Mothers* (Soft Skull Press, 2009) and *My Loves: A Digital Anthology of Queer Love Poems* (Ghost City Press, 2019). Her chapbook, *If I Could Write You a Happier Ending*, is forthcoming from dancing girl press (2021). A graduate of the MFA Writing program at Vermont College of Fine Arts in Montpelier, Mary lives in western Massachusetts with her wife and two children. She is an educator, writer and activist.

Sheri-D Wilson served as Poet Laureate of Calgary 2018–2020. She is the award-winning author of twelve books, the creator of four short films and she has released three albums, which combine music and poetry. Sheri-D has read, performed and taught at festivals across Canada, the United States, the United Kingdom, France, Spain, Belgium, Mexico and South Africa. Recognized for her environmental awareness and activism, she was headliner at the 2014 Emerald Awards, and in 2013, she read with David Suzuki. Her tenth collection of poetry, *Open Letter: Woman against Violence against Women* (Frontenac House, 2014), was short-listed for The Robert Kroetsch Award for Poetry Book of the Year. Her collection *Re:Zoom* (Frontenac House, 2005) won the Stephan G. Stephansson Award for Poetry. In 2017, she received her Doctorate of Letters, honoris causa from Kwantlen University, in Surrey, British Columbia. https://sheridwilson.com/poems/cds/